ASLOM ULLAH

BOYHOOD

A TEENAGE SURVIVAL GUIDE

“Dedicated to my parents because their values helped me through my boyhood years.”

– Aslom Ullah

CONTENTS

Prologue
LIFE IS HARD!

I won't lie to you, dear teenage reader. LIFE'S HARD, like really hard. As you enter into your teenage life, you leave behind the days of innocence and constant play. You will have days of absolute joy when it seems like your whole life is ahead of you and days when your life seems over, like you have literally lost everything. Nobody can prepare you for these years, and you will sometimes find yourself screaming out, "Isn't there some kind of manual or guidebook to all of this?"

The answer to that question: of course there is! Need a survival guide to teenage life? I've got you covered, as you are literally holding it in your hands. I've been both fortunate and equally unfortunate to have lived the life I have lived; I, therefore, thought I would chronicle these for you so you might see patterns and lessons where I did not. Life is episodic, I sometimes find, and I have therefore presented these moments into my life as episodes you can dip in and out of. Do take time to consider the lessons you may draw from my life because, who knows, maybe you will act differently if you find yourself in similar situations in your own teenage life.

Chapter One
CHERISH YOUR PARENTS

Nothing can prepare you for a family death, dear reader, and nobody can ever really tell you how to deal with it, especially when it is the death of a parent and when it happens to you as a teenager. I was barely thirteen years old. It was 6:30 a.m., and it was raining outside. More than anything else, I remember the way it rained – as if the sky itself was crying the tears that would stream down my face uncontrollably in just a few short hours. The rain is what I remember most, and it is the rain that woke me that morning, NOT the telephone call.

My mother and elder brothers had already left the house, and on the telephone, my brother just said, in a flat, monotonous tone, "Come to the hospital...quick. It's Dad." It was enough to make my heart sink and then leap to my throat. I knew something was wrong as things had gone from bad to worse ever since my dad had fallen sick due to his diabetes that year. In all the years that followed, this telephone call has played over and over again in my dreams, in my nightmares.

I don't know about you, dear teenage reader, but I find traumatic events difficult to remember. While I don't remember a lot of the details, I do recall a huge black umbrella. I was barely tall enough to hold it up, but I had to so that I could try my best to shield my younger brothers both from the rain and from the torrential downpour of emotions that overwhelmed us as we neared the hospital doors. Ninth floor. The Intensive Care Unit. I found my paces were quickening and then slowing down at the same time as we neared my father's room. I wanted to know what was wrong, and I also wanted to shut my eyes to what was happening. I heard my brother before I saw him. Still to this day, on the darkest of nights when these memories flood back to me, and I grip my duvet so tight that my fingers whiten, I can hear his muffled words which came out from his hands wherein his face was buried. "He's gone."

You know what, dear teenage reader? I think a small part of me died that day. When my mind registered what he had said, I felt numb. Everything I could hear became one incomprehensible sound, and my vision became blurred. I just stood there. They say brothers sometimes act the same when they find themselves in similar situations, and my brothers all reacted the same way: we just stood there, frozen in our individual spots. I felt like I couldn't move, while everything and everyone around me in that hospital room did.

A nurse came over to my mother and quietly asked how long we needed as a family. "We need to move the body," she said. I hated that nurse in that moment, and I hated what she said. My loving father, who had raised us all and sent us to school, who had played with us on his weekends and given us pocket money for sweets, had with a single word been robbed of all that history and robbed of his humanity. I wanted to scream at her with all my strength and all my might, but I didn't have the energy. Instead, I let out everything I'd been holding in and started to cry right there in the hospital.

The next thing I knew, I was at the graveyard, and we were burying my father at The Gardens of Peace Cemetery. There was a room where they let loved ones say their final goodbyes. When I went to see him, he seemed so peaceful, like he was just resting, the way he'd do on the weekends when we would go and bother him as he tried to sleep in. There was so much I wanted to say to him and also so much I wanted to ask. I'd just become a teenager, and he'd only given me small bits of advice on how to navigate the years ahead. He'd given me zero advice on how to operate in the professional working world because, of course, we were still too young for that. He'd been the centre of my world as a young boy growing up, and it didn't feel real that he was taken when I needed him most.

Even while I was still in my formative years, when I had yet to grow into adulthood, I buried a portion of my childhood along with my beloved father that day. My brothers and I were the first ones to throw handfuls of soil after we lowered him into the ground, and believe me, that was the hardest thing I ever did in my entire life. Throwing the soil onto my beloved father who had been full of life less than a day ago. I think it was at this moment that I realised he was truly gone. The man who never seemed to age a day was suddenly gone. With my father went his encouragement, his kind words, his words of reprimand, and above all else, his laughter. This was what I would miss the most and what I would treasure for the rest of my life.

As a teenager in the 2000s, I did not have the luxury of social media. For us, pictures were taken on a *Kodak* camera, which required the film to be processed in a local pharmacy. You would get the pictures after two to three days, and it was then (and only then) that you would get to see the photo. Due to this, I had very few pictures of or with my father, and the ones I did have were taken at weddings or family visits. For this reason, I treasured those candid pictures I took as a young boy, such as the one I took while he was painting the living room. These pictures and the ones that existed in my head were all that I would have to remember him by.

Adults and teachers always tell you that you should love what you have, but you never really pay any attention to that. I wish I could go back in time and tell my younger self to take more pictures, to spend more time with our dad, and to create more memories with him...but the truth is, even if I could, none of it would be enough. Thus, I tell you, dear teenage reader, that there is never enough time to show the gratitude you have for your parents, and you never really know what you have with them in your life until that presence becomes something you HAD rather than something you still have.

The days that followed were a haze. I sat in my room every day, forcing myself to remember every memory I had of him so that it felt like he was still with me. I remembered the little yellow *Formula 1* race car he'd bought me from the stall in the underground station, the *Power Rangers* toy he'd got me from Church Street Warehouse...and the *Batman and Robin* action figure he'd reluctantly bought me when I was ten because I'd received a bad school report that year.

I should warn you, dear teenager; the thing about forcing memories in that manner is that quite often, bad memories also surface. I remembered the day I had gone with him to have his dialysis done, and I'd been told to stay in the waiting room while he was taken into the ward for the treatment.

That day, *The Sun* newspaper was giving away sunglasses from the new Arnold Schwarzenegger film, *Terminator 3: Rise Of The Machines*, and I'd snuck downstairs to buy a copy of the newspaper from the newsagent. My father told me later that he'd sent a coffee to me from inside but was told, "Your son's gone." I had returned within five minutes, but the damage had been done. My dad sat in dialysis for three hours, thinking his son had left him there.

When the memory resurfaced, I hated myself for being so selfish over something so stupid and childish. I found the sunglasses where I kept my film memorabilia, took them to the kitchen, and put them in the bin. I never wanted to see them ever again.

This was a private moment of grief, and my brothers would tell me later they did similar things. For all of us, we had lost something irretrievable, intangible, and so precious that we felt a sense of disconnect. We grieved, but we grieved alone. There was no sense of collective mourning, perhaps because to mourn together would mean we acknowledged what had happened, and it would make real what we had lost.

I don't know how much time you spend playing *PS5*, dear reader, but our pastime when our father was alive had always been video games. Before *PlayStation* existed, there was the *Super Nintendo* and two-player games you played with friends and family members. When our father was alive, we had spent countless hours playing games like *Street Fighter II, Mortal Kombat, Killer Instinct*, and, of course, the first *Mario Kart*. These 16-bit, 2D games brought joy to our hearts; the musical scores and characters now being etched into our young minds.

In fact, one such game, *Mortal Kombat II*, was linked to our late father. My elder brother was a bit of a collector, and he kept the boxes of video games in pristine condition. So when one of us accidentally stepped on the game's box (definitely not me), he was absolutely livid. He screamed so LOUD, I swear I heard the windows in the living room crack a little. It was only my father who managed to calm him down by telling my brother he would replace the video game box that very day, which he did.

My father never explained how, but he walked into the living room that evening with an empty box for *Mortal Kombat II*, which he proudly handed to my dumbstruck brother. We had always assumed he had just bought the box from a video game shop at a discounted price, but we were wrong.

It would be years later, after his passing, that we would discover among his things…a hidden copy of the video game cartridge; he had bought a brand new copy of the game just to appease my brother and had never told us all the days he was alive.

Thus, following his passing, the *Super Nintendo* no longer bought us any comfort or solace. It was just another reminder of him and of his selfless act of kindness. Sometimes, as teenagers or even children, we may overlook something our parents have done for us as we go about our busy lives. It may be the blanket they place on us when we have fallen asleep on the sofa, some dinner they leave for us in the fridge because we have decided to go out with our friends, or replacing a crushed video game box by purchasing a whole new game. What I am asking, dear reader, is for you to look out for these things because I learnt the hard way that these actions exist, and neither my brothers nor I ever really got the chance to show our gratitude for them the way that we would now. You, dear reader, have the chance to look for these hidden gems as you navigate your teenage years and express your gratitude and thanks to your parents for what they do for you out of love behind your back.

Chapter Two
NEVER PICK A FIGHT WITH A TANK

The next episode I want to tell you about is from a year later and is a little more lighthearted. I was still processing my father's death, but the normality of school life helped me to get through it, almost automatically slotting me into teenage life. I was fourteen years old, in Year Nine and decided I would pick a fight with a tank. His name was Abdullah, and he literally looked like *WWE* superstar *Triple H*, except he had black hair. I still regret starting that fight, but maybe after I've told you about it, you will realise why I did, as poorly advised as my decision was.

It was June, and the last two lessons of school on a Friday. I was in Year Nine, but I was SO ready for Year Ten. Being June and nearly the end of the academic year, we were all exhausted and not looking forward to playing basketball. Unfortunately, that was what we were scheduled to play that term. Our P.E. teacher, Mr Dillon, was a slave-driver too. Now, you'd think that, being a physical education teacher, he'd have the stamina of footballer Cristiano Ronaldo and the physique of Dwayne Johnson, right? Wrong. Mr Dillon was a lazy man who was out of shape and never put the work in himself. Now, don't get me wrong, dear teenage reader. I'm not shaming him in any way. It was just the hypocrisy of it all that annoyed me. He'd spend hours telling us how fit he was in the past and how, "Back in my day, we'd run 10K and not even break a sweat." Yeah, right. "Go on then, run 10K now, Mr Dillon, I dare you," I'd think to myself. He never did, but that didn't stop him from torturing us on a weekly basis, trust me.

It was during one of these torture sessions on the basketball court that I bumped into Abdullah (or 'Triple H' to be more precise). Nobody messed with him because nobody had a death wish, plain and simple. I didn't have any desire to be beaten to a pulp either, but on the basketball court, it was pretty hard not to bump into him as he was just so big. I accidentally bounced off him when I collided with him. He took this personally. I mean, I apologised, but he was having none of it. He wanted to get me back, and he did. This was how it went down:

I was preparing to shoot a lay-up, but as I took the second step, I was in mid-air, and I felt the ground shake under me. He was charging at me like a rhino, and (being suspended in the air) there was little I could do. He crashed right into me, and I swear it felt like a train had hit me. I fell to the ground, hard. I felt my rib twist inwards as 'Triple H' bulldozed into me, sending me flying across the court. My sneakers screeched me to a halt when they hit the floor.

The whistle from lazy Mr Dillon brought the game to a standstill, and I was given a penalty shot. I didn't score it, probably because my ribs were killing me. The rest of the game played out without any drama, and I waited until the end of the lesson to get my sweet revenge.

After we all changed back into our school uniforms, Mr Dillon released us, and the class headed downstairs to registration. I watched Abdullah with rage burning in my eyes as he headed out of the school gymnasium. Revenge was all that ran through my mind. I picked up a basketball and walked out behind him, treading silently so that he did not hear my steps.

Before we reached the stairs leading down to our Form room, I threw the basketball at the back of Abdullah's head. I'm not sure what I expected. Perhaps I hoped it would knock him out or that the unexpected nature of the blow might bring tears to his eyes. I also hoped that he would not know it was me who had thrown it (I mean, it could have been anyone who threw the basketball, right? RIGHT?)

In reality, it did not play out the way that I had naively hoped. Instead, Abdullah stopped dead in his tracks. He took a dramatic pause and slowly turned on his heels. His shoulders were hunched, and he had this distorted look on his face, the kind of look you get when you go into a public bathroom and open the cubicle to find someone else's poop inside the toilet. That's how he saw me: someone else's poop that he would instantly flush.

Abdullah marched towards me, grabbed me by the collar, lifted me up and dragged me down the stairs. My feet remained in the air, and I was helpless. He was so strong that I felt like one of those used cars on a scrap heap being picked up by a giant claw in order to be dropped into the metal teeth of a car crusher. When he reached the bottom of the stairs, he stopped and SLAMMED me against the wall. His distorted face had by now become even more contorted. I swear to you, it was so painful that it felt like when I hit the wall, my soul temporarily bounced out of my body, saw his ugly face, and then jumped right back into my body.

The basketball knockout had been my whole plan of attack, and I was now on the defensive. I had no plan, especially as he was a hulking brute of a guy. He raised his tree trunk of an arm to rain down punches on me, but thankfully, at that very moment, the Head of Year, Mr Stone, yelled two words that probably saved my life: "Boys, STOP!" He ran over and pushed Abdullah off me. He then told me to wait outside his office.

Abdullah was suspended for a week for his behaviour on and off the court, and I was given three days of after-school detention for 'inappropriate use of a basketball'. I know, dear reader. It was completely appropriate, if you asked me, and I am pretty sure even the legendary Michael Jordan would have approved. However, my attack did little to hurt 'Triple H' and almost resulted in me getting a bloody nose or even worse.

That might be the lesson for you, dear teenage reader. In those wildlife documentaries on television, you wouldn't see a rhino attack a deer and then see that deer throw a pebble at the rhino. No deer is that stupid! Staying on the animal analogy, you could say I literally poked the bear, and the bear nearly flattened me to a pulp after dragging me down the stairs. My advice? Don't start a fight you cannot finish, dear reader and never, ever poke a bear if you value your life.

Chapter Three

ALWAYS COVER YOUR TRACKS!

Have you ever ALMOST burnt your entire house down and then attempted to cover your tracks, only to be caught out on a technicality by your mum, who used the FBI skills she probably learnt at 'Parent Academy'? If you have, then you know what I am talking about. If not, then strap yourselves in because this episode is literally FIRE in every sense of the word...

Two months after the fight with 'Abdullah the Tank', this incident would occur. I was just over fourteen years old, and THE INTERNET had just come out. Let me tell you, dear teenage reader, it was the most exciting thing to enter into a child's house since the television and the Super Nintendo. To us back then, it was like some kind of strange artificial intelligence. When you connected to the internet, your computer became a sort of gateway to this insane supercomputer out there that knew EVERYTHING.

We didn't have *Google* back then. Instead, we had a website called *Ask Jeeves*, which I think has now become *Ask.com*. Back then, Jeeves was presented as a sort of butler and was a man in a suit to whom you could ask anything.

The only problem was that the internet back then was dial-up. Booting it up was extremely slow and laborious, and the computer would make a weird telephone-like sound when it connected to the internet. While this would probably annoy the HELL out of you, we didn't mind it and considered it part of the process of going online. This might sound a bit of a random fact to tell you now, but trust me, it is important to this episode.

Context out of the way, let me tell you what happened that Saturday – a day when all dreadful things seem to happen to me. Seriously, there have been some Saturdays I would just SLEEP through just to avoid the dreadful thing that was probably going to happen to me later in the day.

I'm getting sidetracked. So, it was a Saturday afternoon, and my mum, dad and brothers had all gone out to *IKEA* to buy a new television stand. *IKEA* was about forty minutes away, and the shop itself was huge, taking about thirty minutes to navigate. Taking into consideration the forty minutes they would take driving back, that gave me just under two hours at home to surf the Web. I could not WAIT to download and play SO many games through the internet. Before I did, I decided that the first thing I wanted to do was to make myself an omelette, sunny-side up. I would have this with some toast while browsing the World Wide Web. I headed into the kitchen, turned on the cooker, put some oil in a frying pan, and let it heat. I knew this would take a while, so I thought I'd go and boot up the internet on the computer in the living room.

As I turned on the computer, my mind filled with all the things I would search for. At the very top of my list was a *Batman Returns* ROM file, which could be played on a *Super Nintendo* emulator. I had heard that you could now play *SNES* games on your PC for free with an emulator, and just thinking about it made me giddy. I mean, imagine...I could play ANY *SNES* game – even the ones we'd just heard about on that television show *GamesMaster,* but were unavailable in our local store.

The internet took its merry time to connect, making that strange dial-up sound I had become so familiar with. As soon as I got the connection, I headed to *Ask Jeeves* and began downloading the ROM for *Batman Returns* along with the emulator. Even though each of these was only a few megabytes, the estimated time to download them was around ten minutes.

I just sat and waited and waited and waited. As I waited some more, I caught a faint whiff of my mother's cooking. It smelt like she was frying samosas. "Oooh...samosas. I could definitely do with a few of them," I thought to myself. Mum usually makes some and brings them round to us in the living room, so I thought I'd just wait for her to do that. I know what you're thinking – and you're right, but I was a child, and my mind wandered easily. A whole minute would go by before I would remember that my mother wasn't at home, and what I was smelling was the oil burning in the frying pan I'd left on the cooker.

I BOLTED to the kitchen, flung the door open, and there it was: the 'Oil Volcano'. The oil had caught fire and had grown tall like a volcano. It looked as if it was breathing, and the top of this frying pan fire had actually reached the ceiling. It was heaving, growing...it even sounded like it was angry. "FIRE!" I thought, and my thoughts immediately turned to my primary school science lessons where we learnt about different types of fire and how to put them out. I remembered my teacher, Miss Durrant, telling me, "Some fires you put out with water, but not fires containing oil as water makes them worse. You need sand for that, especially a grease fire in a frying pan." Well, I was a child in a house in London. I had NO access to sand, and the fire was literally rising. "Sorry, Miss Durrant," I whispered to myself, but water was going to have to do.

Covering my mouth with one hand, I ran into the kitchen and filled the nearest jug with water with the other. I went to the door, preparing my course of action. I decided I needed to be smart about this, so I rehearsed what I would do: I would throw the water at the grease fire volcano, quick-turn, and then jump through the kitchen doorway, closing the door behind me with my foot. I rehearsed it in my head a few times until it seemed like it was a flawless plan. All the while, the fire spread across the cooker.

I decided it was now or never. I did just as I rehearsed: I THREW the water onto the frying pan, and as the water made contact with the pan, I saw the flame enlarge right before my eyes. It was without blinking that I quick-turned, jumped through the kitchen doorway, and used the tip of my foot to pull the door closed behind me.

There was a loud BANG, and I waited five whole agonising minutes before I DARED open that kitchen door again. I was terrified about what I'd find. Had I burnt the kitchen to a crisp? Would I need to replace all the silverware, plates and pans? As I peeped through the door, I realised that, fortunately, I'd done nothing of the sort. I saw that the kitchen was still intact and everything was where it should be. The frying pan, however, was not so lucky. It was burnt to a crisp, and its handle was nowhere to be seen. I guessed that this was the explosion I'd heard from outside.

Seeing as the kitchen was still intact, I realised that the situation was actually salvageable. All I had to do was clean up the cooker and replace the frying pan – my parents would never know that I'd unleashed HELL in the kitchen. It was 4:30 p.m., and the local hardware shop, *One Price*, closed at 5 p.m. I had thirty minutes to get there and buy a new frying pan. There was no time to waste. I grabbed my trainers and my wallet and headed out. 'Operation Frying Pan' was officially underway.

My time outside the house was pretty much a frenzied dash. I remember grabbing a frying pan that looked like the one I had destroyed, paying for it and then running back home. The whole ordeal lasted about twenty minutes. I wasn't sure how long I had to complete 'Operation Frying Pan', but I knew that it was not long. The first order of business was making the frying pan LOOK like it was used and not brand new. I, therefore, put some butter onto it and heated it up for about two minutes. Using a knife, I then weathered the bottom a little bit, adding some dents and scratches. "Good as old," I thought, smiling to myself as I placed it back inside the cupboard. Mum will never know the difference.

I then proceeded to clean the cooker, which was covered in soot and oil. I cleaned the counter and the floor. As I was cleaning the sink, I heard some commotion at the front door: they were back.

I gracefully walked out of the kitchen, switched off the computer by holding down the power-button, picked up the television magazine, and sat on the sofa. Disaster averted. In my mind, I was given an award from the London Fire Brigade for my quick-thinking and bravery.

When my mum walked in, she threw off her coat and headed for the kitchen. I'm not much of a swimmer because I can't hold my breath for very long, but as she stepped through that door, I held my breath for about sixty seconds. TRUST ME ON THAT. I kept my breath held as she used the sink and turned on the cooker to warm some food. I half expected her to scream my name in anger or shout something along the lines of, "Who the HELL burnt down the kitchen?" But she never did. 'Operation Frying Pan' had been a HUGE success.

It continued to remain a success that entire week, and Mum would even use that old-looking-new frying pan to make me some omelettes. All was well, and all was forgotten.

That is until my nosy-neighbour Morty decided to pay my mum a visit. You see, we had this neighbour who would visit my mum every weekend to chat about life. I mean, she was old, so God knows how much LIFE she had left to talk about. I have four brothers, and the worst thing was Morty ALWAYS asked about us 'boys' and wanted a full update on how we were doing at school, if we'd had any fights between us, and if we were keeping up with our chores. I half expected her to turn up to our parent-teacher meetings!

Anyway, that Saturday (a week after 'Operation Frying Pan's MONUMENTAL success), Morty popped by for her weekly 'catch-up'. She spent the whole afternoon sitting on her designated chair in the kitchen. Oh, did I not tell you? SHE HAD HER OWN CHAIR IN OUR KITCHEN. I mean, the absolute audacity of it all!

The issue arose as she was leaving. She leaned against the wall with the palm of her hand in order to hoist herself up, and when she took away her hand, she noticed a small amount of soot on it. The walls. Those darn walls. I'd forgotten to clean the walls! I'd done the sink, the floor, the counter, bought a whole new frying pan and aged it, but I'd overlooked the way soot gathers on walls. Why? Because THEY DIDN'T TELL US IN OUR SCHOOL SCIENCE LESSONS THAT SOOT GATHERS ON WALLS AFTER A FIRE! Thanks, Miss Durrant. Thanks a lot.

Morty haughtily told my mum, "You really SHOULD clean these walls occasionally like I do, at least once a week." Now, my mum was VERY house-proud and was not about to let some neighbour tell her how to maintain her house.

"What did you say? Are you insinuating that I don't clean my house?" She was mortified. Mortified with 'Haughty Morty'.

My mum then touched the wall herself and noticed the soot. She then proceeded to analyse it, going from the wall to the cooker to the shelf below. She picked up the frying pan and noticed it seemed to look both old and new at the same time. She then used her FBI analysis skills to figure out just who it was that burnt her frying pan, covered the wall in soot and replaced it, hoping she would not notice what had happened.

To this day, I have no idea how she figured out it was me and not one of my brothers because she didn't come and ask us one by one, like she usually does, fishing for clues. Nope. Not this time. This time, she simply called out my name, adding, "DID YOU BURN DOWN THE KITCHEN AND THINK I WOULD NOT NOTICE? NO COMPUTER ACCESS FOR A WEEK!"

No access to the computer meant no internet access, which meant no Super Nintendo games. She knew how to hurt me, and she knew what she was doing. I told you – FBI agent.

You might be wondering, sceptical teenage reader, where the lesson is in all this. Am I advising you not to leave a frying pan full of oil on the cooker while you go sauntering off to play on the internet? ABSOLUTELY, but then you already knew that. You also know not to throw water at a grease-fire because, at this stage in your teenage life, I'm sure someone has told you this, too. My advice, teenage reader, is DO NOT lie to your parents. Firstly, because it's immoral and lying only breeds more lies. However, I will add that if there is ever a situation where you have done something terrible like dropping a plate by accident (nothing as ridiculous as setting a frying pan on fire, which will probably apply to 1% of all the readers of this book), then always cover your tracks and leave NOTHING to chance, because parents are the BEST detectives.

I swear to you (and this is not just me talking about the frying pan incident), parents can LITERALLY get to the bottom of an incident if you're not careful. Let's say you accidentally knock over a vase: when your parents visit the crime scene, it's almost as if they can blink their eyes and dramatically reconstruct the incident, with the vase being put back together in their imagination. This 'parent-vision' then allows them to watch a ghostly version of you knock it over, grabbing the shelf as you do, where you leave a fingerprint linking you to the crime.

If you don't want to get caught like I did, leave NO stone unturned and wash down all surfaces for fingerprints, DNA traces and the like. Do not leave a SHARD of evidence, as even a small fragment of glass at the bottom of your trainers from that vase you stupidly dropped can be used to link you to the crime. Also, make sure you have an AIRTIGHT alibi for the time of the incident, preferably far away from your house, with someone who can corroborate your story of being away from home when the vase disappeared.

All parents, every single one of them, have probably attended 'Parent Academy' because every single one of them KNOWS WHAT'S UP – each and every time. Cover your tracks. Have an alibi and always try to cast suspicion on another sibling, preferably a baby brother or sister that cannot talk yet but can walk.

Chapter Four

NEVER KEEP FIREWORKS IN YOUR WARDROBE

"Remember, remember the 5th of November..." Fireworks are great, aren't they? You see them on New Year's Day on the TV, being used all over the world to welcome in the New Year. That said, I do think people nowadays have actually forgotten the reason we celebrate 'Bonfire Night' and the fact that it dates back to when Guy Fawkes was caught trying to blow up Parliament with gunpowder and was subsequently tortured until he confessed. Not many people know how, in the aftermath of this, Parliament declared the 5th of November a national holiday, with fireworks being used to celebrate the fact that Guy Fawkes and his co-conspirators failed to use gunpowder in the way that they had planned. Thus, the nursery rhyme reads, "Remember, remember the 5th of November, Gunpowder, Treason and Plot."

I'm getting sidetracked, of course, as always. The topic of this episode IS fireworks, though, and when I was a kid in Year Nine, fireworks were a great way to have fun with your friends. Only specific newsagents would sell fireworks, though, and you had to take someone who was eighteen or older to buy them for you. Something about them being a safety risk?

Due to this, our parents only ever bought us sparklers and NEVER let us go out on Bonfire Night. This is because, back then, it was actually dangerous to be out on the streets. I mean, you could literally be shot at in a firework drive-by. One of the most popular fireworks at the time were Roman candles. You were meant to place Roman candles upright in the grass and light them, watching them fire shots into the air. Teenagers being teenagers, the youngsters of our generation found other more dangerous uses for these fireworks very quickly. Teens would wrap up their hands with the sleeves of their hoodies and hold Roman candles like sawn-off shotguns, firing them at each other or even at bystanders foolish enough to be out after 7 p.m. on the 5th of November. The story I am about to narrate to you, however, did not happen on the 5th of November, oh no. It happened the day before.

I still don't know why to this day, but my elder brother kept his fireworks in his wardrobe rather than in a metal biscuit tin, as we had been advised at school. I had no knowledge he had stored them in this way...that is until I heard a BANG, followed by another BANG one afternoon as I flicked through the TV channels to see what was on.

I was home alone (again) and in the living room. I could hear the sounds coming from my elder brother's room. I crept towards the door. This is because all of us younger brothers were BFL (Banned For Life) and had signed contracts to that effect, promising never to go in without permission.

This situation, however, seemed to stand as an exception, so I slowly opened the door and kicked it open with all my strength. Why did I kick it, you ask? Well, I kicked it open because I realised the fireworks had (due to the intense heat of being in a wardrobe in a room with a closed door) gone off. The bangers had gone off first, and they'd lit the Roman candles, which were now on the floor of the wardrobe, taking shots at the clothes above. It was like some nightmare comedy sketch that I could not wake up from. Worst of all, a small fire had started at the base of the wardrobe.

"FIRE!" I thought, and again, my first thoughts turned to putting the fire out. So far, the fire was small — only a few t-shirts were ablaze. The Ralph Lauren designer wear, the Calvin Klein jeans, and the Armani jackets hanging at the top were still untouched by the flames. The same went for my brother's formal beige suit, which was still standing proud on the railing. There was still time to save the day!

I ran to the bathroom and began filling the biggest bucket we had. Now, I don't know about your bathroom taps, dear reader, but mine were EXTREMELY slow. The water came out EVER so slowly. I think about three minutes went by before the bucket was completely filled.

When I returned to the bedroom with the bucket, I was no longer staring down a small fire at the base of the wardrobe. Oh no. The fire had grown and had now engulfed the entire wardrobe. The whole thing was completely ablaze. All the branded clothes were now <u>properly</u> alight, and the fire seemed to be growing even larger.

I THREW the bucket of water at the centre of the fire, and in an instant, most of it went out. There was a loud sizzle when the water hit the fire, and I won't lie, this was quite satisfying to watch and to hear, almost like ASMR. I had to do this one more time for the remaining flames to be put out, and the job was done. Unfortunately, so too was the damage. Nothing had escaped the fire, and my brother's entire collection of designer clothing was now a pile of soot. The beige suit was now charcoal black with some beige highlights. I sighed with relief but also with disappointment. Yes, I'd put the fire out, but I'd not managed to save a single item of clothing from being destroyed.

It dawned on me that while I had put out the fire, I hadn't taken the best course of action. The smart thing to do would have been to remove all the designer wear from the room FIRST before attempting to put out the fire. EVACUATING the clothes, if you will. It's like if there's a fire in a building, you wouldn't hear the fire-fighters say, "Everyone stay calm and stay where you are, we are dealing with the fire. If you find yourself coughing or see your arm has caught on fire, do not be alarmed, as this is perfectly normal." No. The fire-fighters evacuate everyone FIRST and then deal with the fire. Lesson learnt, I guess?

When my elder brother got home that evening, I had to tell a little white lie and inform him that when I went into the room, the wardrobe was completely ablaze. I did not tell him that there had been a chance to rescue some of his expensive designer clothes; I didn't have a death wish. So, dear teenage reader, please learn from my mistake. If you ever discover a small (I mean it, SMALL) fire in your house, before you try putting it out, evacuate all people and designer clothing out of the room.

Chapter Five

DON'T PLAY WITH YOUR FOOD

I don't know about you, but I've always taken my eyesight for granted. I mean, blinking is a bit like breathing, and it's probably one of the few things we do without thinking, just as we sometimes touch our eyes without thinking it through. Got a little itch on the corner of your eye? Just give it a rub, and it will be better! You never consider what your hands may have touched beforehand. Well, you never consider it until it's too late.

This was my fate one Saturday (I told you, they are the WORST) afternoon when I was in Year Nine. I was watching television and slowly eating two delicious butter croissants, which I'd propped beside me, washing them down with a *Pepsi*. As I watched TV, I felt an itch in my right eye. I decided it just needed a little rub. With a few crumbs of the buttery croissant still on my fingers, I touched my eye, and one of those devilish bits of croissant got into my eye. At first, I didn't realise, but a few seconds later, as I started to blink, I felt like something was definitely in my eye, and it wasn't going away, no matter how much I blinked.

I ran immediately to the bathroom and threw water on my face like my eyesight depended on it. I dabbed it with a towel. "Job done," I thought. Wrong. Now, my eye was sore and started to hurt. It felt like there was a tiny pebble inside my eye, and I noticed it every time I blinked.

I. Felt. It. Every. Single. Time.

I told my mum I needed to go to the Western Eye Hospital on Marylebone Road IMMEDIATELY as I was literally about to go blind! Unfortunately, my mum replied with, "Gosh, you're so dramatic it's unreal". Me, being dramatic? She was, of course, unaware of the gravity of the situation: there was bread stuck in my eye, and unless we acted quickly, skin was going to form on top of the crumb, and I would feel that tiny pebble each and every time I blinked for the rest of my natural existence. If left untreated, it may well even lead to permanent blindness. Yes, dear reader, jumping to conclusions was my speciality back then.

If I wanted to be seen by an eye doctor that night, I realised I was going to have to take drastic action and fast. I decided to take matters into my own hands. As I was depositing my night-time tea into the magical sink where cups had just washed themselves and found their way to the shelf, I deliberately bumped into the kitchen door. "Watch out", was my mum's response, to which I replied, "Sorry, it's just a bit blurry, but it's fine." Holding my mug in my left hand, I then deliberately started pretending to fumble with my right hand as if I couldn't find the sink. My mum stood there, folding her arms in a sceptical manner. She wasn't buying it, I realised. It's tough acting blind, trust me on that, especially in front of your mum, who knows all your tricks. In order to sell this act, I would have to sustain some sort of further injury. I, therefore, turned on the hot water tap on purpose and put my hand under it to 'wash' the mug. My scream forced my mum to unfold her arms and rush over with such maternal concern that even I thought I'd done it by accident.

"Oh my God, you really can't see! You accidentally turned on the hot tap instead of the cold one, you poor thing!"

She forced my hand under the cold tap and rinsed it, during which I told her, "It's Okay, Mum, I guess it will be fine in the morning..."

"Absolutely not, I'm taking you there now myself. Get your coat."

The next thing I knew, I was sitting in the emergency room of the Western

Eye Hospital, and it was pretty grim, let me tell you. I thought my injury was bad, but this was something else. While I was sitting there with a bit of a crumb in my eye, there was one guy with a bandage over both eyes wearing a cool pair of *Ray-Ban* sunglasses, and the guy sat across from him had an eyepatch on as if he'd just walked off a pirate ship for his weekly check-up.

I sat there for about an hour while the doctor saw to 'Mr *Ray-Ban*' and 'Captain Jack Sparrow'. I was eventually seen at around midnight. It was by a doctor who gave me the 'are you serious?' look when he saw me.

Apparently, A&E is for trauma patients only, and a breadcrumb in the eye did not count as trauma. He looked like a skin-coloured Shrek, so I don't know what his problem was, and honestly, it traumatised me a tiny bit, too. He had a little look at my eye with a pocket-light and said he found nothing. I asked him to look again, but *Shrek* sent me home, telling me to get some sleep.

I did sleep that night, but I had the worst nightmare. In it, I was blind, but I'd been blind for a while. A few years had passed since I'd been blinded by a croissant in this nightmare. I also had a glass eye, which I put in my eye socket every morning. I would take this glass eye out of a wooden box under my bed, where I had a whole collection of glass eyeballs – one for every occasion. There was a regular eye, but also an eyeball with a smiley face on it, a red demon-eye, and an eye that had a *magic 8-ball* in it. It was like I was some *James Bond* villain, let me tell you, and not the good kind. I would change my eyeball according to my mood, and if I planned to have a pleasant day, I would wear the smiley-face eyeball. Don't you DARE ask me what the *magic 8-ball* eye was for! I mean, I know it was my dream, but I can't explain that.

Anyway, I woke up at 8 a.m. that Sunday morning, profusely sweating and stressed out of my mind. It still felt like there was that same tiny pebble in my eye, and I was convinced that some skin had formed on top of the little crumb. It needed to be cut out with a little scalpel by an expert.

No time to talk to parents this time or play blind. I got dressed while my entire family slept and hailed a black cab down back to the Western Eye Hospital.

Sitting in the A&E once again, it felt like déjà vu, let me tell you. This time, the other characters in my little episode were different, however. There were three women with dark glasses, an old man holding his eye (his hand was ON his eye; he wasn't literally holding his eyeball) and a man in a wheelchair with nothing that seemed to be wrong with his eyes.

When I was finally called, I had already started to mentally choose the kind of eyepatch I wanted to cover the eye the doctor was probably going to slice open. I'd settled on black leather so that it would match all my outfits. Black goes with everything, they say, and so that was the colour I chose for my eyepatch.

Dr Meridian, a brunette doctor in her mid-twenties, was the doctor who was going to see me. She reminded me of one of my primary school teachers. Dr Meridian smiled when I instructed her to just cut the eyeball out, saying, "I'm the doctor, not you, young man, so I will be the one giving the instructions." She asked me to lean back, and I did as I was told.

She told me she would be placing a special dye in my eye to help her see if there were any foreign objects in it. "Don't move or blink now, or you WILL lose that eye." I kept my eye open so hard, I swear I thought it was going to pop out.

She leaned in with something that looked like a long cotton bud (the ones people use to clean out their ears) and dabbed it on my eye. "Got it!" she exclaimed. She sat me up and showed me the tiny little crumb, now covered in some of my eye's fluid.

The feeling of a tiny little pebble in my eye was gone, and I could finally blink normally. I was so ecstatic I screamed, "Oh my God, thank you! I could hug you, I swear! The night doctor told me there was nothing there but you...you managed to..."

She smiled broadly. "That's why we're the doctors on duty during the day, and they are the night doctors." I didn't know what she meant, nor did I care. I was just relieved beyond measure that I got to keep the eye and didn't have to invest in a glass eye set or an eye patch.

You may find yourself in my position one day, dear reader, as you navigate your way through your teenage years. By that, I mean sitting on a sofa having a snack, such as a slice of pizza, a sandwich or even a croissant. If and when you do find yourself in such a position, I implore you, do not touch your eye immediately after putting down that naughty little snack. It may almost cost you your eye.

Chapter Six

AVOID JUMPING ONTO A MOVING BUS

I can imagine what you're thinking, avid teenage reader. "Great, a filler episode about a boring school trip that somehow ended badly." You're wondering if this episode is like one of those episodes on a *Netflix* series, existing only to bring the total number of episodes to a respectable number. In response to your thoughts, I will state that the trip started badly rather than ending terribly and that this is by no means a filler episode. I wish it was. I wish that the school trip had been mundane and boring rather than beginning in the death-defying way that it did.

I was halfway through Year Nine at the time, approaching the grand-old age of fourteen. The night before the trip, I'd stayed up playing *Soul Blade*, which is a precursor to the *Soul Calibur* series your generation may have heard of. *Soul Blade* was a sword-fighting game on the first *PlayStation*, and it had an absolutely KILLER soundtrack. Hell, I'd play the game just to watch the intro because the intro was absolutely legendary.

It was because I'd spent all night cutting down enemies in *Soul Blade* that I woke up late that morning. It was 8:30 a.m. when I rolled off my bed, and I had thirty minutes to get showered, dressed, and sat at my desk, ready to say "Present" in my normal, zombie-like registration voice.

The class trip that day was to the Imperial War Museum in South London. We were told that we would be visiting a life-size trench from World War I and come face-to-face with a military tank from the same period – even getting the chance to step inside it. I was a teenager and told I would get the chance to sit in a tank. I was sold. I HAD to be on this trip.

I got showered and dressed so fast that I set a new record that day: three minutes and thirty seconds. If you ever want to do this, dear reader, then let me give you some tips: the aim is to dry off with a towel, step out of your shower with your right foot and use that same foot to step INTO your trousers.

My shirt was washed, but it hadn't dried yet. It was freezing cold outside, as always. I needed the clothes to be dried instantly and didn't have time to waste fumbling with a washing machine. My solution to this impossible situation? Well, let's just say it was a stroke of sheer genius. I threw the shirt into the microwave and nuked it, placing a Pop-Tart (my breakfast) on top.

When I came hobbling in from the shower, jumping into my trousers fully, I saw that the microwave had beeped. Perfect. Shirt and breakfast were ready. I threw the shirt on, popped the Pop-Tart between my teeth, and headed for my shoes. It was the late 1990s, so *Velcro* straps all the way. After socks, of course.

I headed out, doing up my shirt as I stepped into the cold of the March morning. It was 8:45 a.m. I was going to make it. The class was due to leave at 9:10 a.m., so realistically, I had about twenty minutes before the class would make their way out of the building. The bus to school took around eighteen minutes to reach the school. This meant I HAD to get the first available bus.

I was walking as quickly as I could to the bus stop, eating my Pop-Tart as I did, occasionally taking it out so I could chew on the bit I'd bitten off. As I hurriedly walked up to the bust stop, I saw that a bus had JUST arrived. Perfect, I thought. I quickened my pace even more, and this fast-walk turned into a RUN when I saw the bus was leaving me (and my hopes of sitting in that tank) behind. Not today.

I bolted after the bus and JUMPED onto it. Now, I have to explain what kind of bus this was. It wasn't one of the modern London buses where you get in and tap your Oyster card. Oh no. This was one of those old buses from the 1990s, which had an open back compartment with a pole you could hold onto as you ascended the bus. On those buses, you didn't talk to the driver at all; instead, you paid a conductor the fare you owed. You might see those being used to host weddings nowadays, and I think they have this kind of afternoon-tea event on one of these buses, too.

Anyway, I JUMPED into the bus and grabbed the pole. The only problem (and I blame myself entirely for this) was that my *Velcro* school shoes had ZERO grip underneath. I lost my footing. I slipped all the way to the bottom, and I was holding onto that pole for DEAR LIFE. The driver was completely unaware of what was happening, and the conductor was upstairs collecting fares. As the bus increased its speed, it was like my heartbeat was quickening to try and catch up. The other passengers looked on in horror at this teenager (me) who was being dragged across the road, holding onto the torn reigns of a wild horse!

Now, you might be wondering, curious teenage reader, why on God's good earth I refused to LET GO. Well, let me enlighten you as to my thought process at the time. I could see and hear the other cars behind the bus. They were just at my heels. I knew that if I let go of that pole, the cars behind the bus – all of which were going at the same speed of about 20mph – would absolutely FLATTEN me. Holding on was my only hope of living, and I prayed that the bus would stop in traffic.

It was a full two minutes of me holding onto that pole, screaming in an undignified way before the bus reached the next stop. When the bus finally stopped, I let out a sigh of relief and a small, wimpy cough. I'd inhaled a LOT of the smoke from all the cars as well as the bus, and the fresh smell of burning rubber was well inside my lungs. Trust me on that.

When I stood up, I expected a loud cheer from all the passengers. I got no applause or a standing ovation. Instead, this little old lady who had the best seat for the whole spectacle simply said, "What the HELL is the matter with you? Look at what you've done to yourself."

I looked down at my school uniform. It was in absolute tatters. The trousers were in pieces and looked like someone had taken a machete to them.

The blazer had somehow burnt around the bottom edges, and my shirt was covered in dirt and grit. The tie must have somehow got lodged in something and came off during the whole ordeal, as it was no longer tied around my neck.

Do you want to know the irony of it all? A second bus pulled up right behind me just as I was flattening out my shirt. There was no need for all the heroics and stupidity, after all. The conductor of the first bus refused to let me on after all my antics on the back of his bus, and I ended up taking that second bus to school. The driver of that bus was even nice enough to let me ride the bus for free. His kind words as I embarked on the bus have remained with me all these years: "Next time, son, just let go."

I arrived at 9:05 a.m. at the school and ran into the tutor room. I'd made it, or so I thought. My Humanities teacher, Mr Harbone, took one look at me in my battered uniform and told me categorically that I would not be allowed to come on the trip looking like that, adding, "Listen here, if you think I'm taking you to a museum, where you will be representing the school, looking like THAT, you've got another thing coming."

I ended up risking my life just to stay in school and do History worksheets. 'The Harbonator' had a whole folder full of them (because he's a loser), and I guessed he made them in his spare time because he had no social life.

So, teenage reader, heed my lesson. I mean, there are probably several lessons here, but the one that seemed to stick with me was pointlessly holding onto that bus when there was one right behind me. Maybe the bus could be a metaphor for bigger or at least other things. During your teenage years, life will always take some things away, but there may be other, better things waiting for you that you aren't aware of or you can't see because you're too busy holding onto the thing that's leaving. While you should hold onto the things you love, don't hold on too tightly to the things that are leaving you, at least not forcefully so. This is especially the case when it's time to move on, and you're holding on just for the sake of it. Like that bus driver said, sometimes, it's best just to let go.

Chapter Seven

NEVER TRY TO ESCAPE SCHOOL

I hate Sports Day. I always have, ever since I was in primary school. I hated it even more in secondary school. I know what you're going to say, dear teenage reader: "the activities are so fun, and it's a break from the regular, lame timetable." Yes, it is, but you didn't do sports day at the tail end of Year Nine at my school. If you had, then, like me, you would have compared it to that other institution adults are sent to as a form of punishment – PRISON.

That year, the headmaster decided to oversee Sports Day. God only knows why. He'd had this mid-life crisis or something and suddenly decided he would prioritise fitness across the school (as if that would somehow suck in his pot-belly we could all see hanging out). I swear, I felt sorry for his belt. It looked like it was trying its best to hold his pot-belly in and could burst at any second.

Anyway, that year, he put in strict rules, and let me tell you, it was torture. We had to come into school in our P.E. kit – a horrible green shirt and shorts that looked like they had been passed down five generations.

We were not allowed to bring our own packed lunches either, oh no. We had to eat these 'healthy' lunches the school had prepared. Lukewarm, stale salad with no cucumber, quinoa, hardened meatballs (which were apparently good sources of protein), and a sinister orange juice. Why was it sinister? Well, the expiry date on each bottle had been scratched off, so for all we knew, it was expired orange juice that was bought in bulk with a 90% discount from the local grocery shop. Judging by the meatballs, they were probably made from the rats that had been caught in the school canteen. And quinoa? Yeah, right.

After doing two relay races, the long-jump and the high-jump (where my head hit the pole – don't you dare ask), I was DONE with Sports Day. I told my friends there was no way I was going to suffer any further, and I was going to make a run for it.

The school had put in a strict policy that no students were allowed to leave school premises that day, and teachers were given high-visibility vests and allocated stations to guard. There were teachers guarding the front doors, the fire-escape, the gates, and the car park. I bet Alcatraz had fewer guards than we did! Some of the teachers took their roles so seriously that they marched up and down their designated posts like NPCs in a video game.

All the students were in the school playground, and the school was locked down pretty tightly...but I knew something nobody else knew. The far wall of the playground overlooked a small, dingy alley that led to the main road. Nobody was guarding it, not a single teacher. I decided this was my route. This was how I would initiate the school's first 'prison break'.

As the wall was in the school's playground, I needed a distraction, and quite a big one. I needed a student that teachers absolutely trusted without a shadow of a doubt to provide this distraction – and I knew just who to ask.

My friend Ali has never told a lie in his life. I don't think he even knew HOW to lie, and this would work in my favour. Ali was a straight-A student, and every one of his teachers counted on him to always know the answer to any question. In all manner of nerd, Ali was the golden goose. I walked up to Ali and told him what he had to do: "Take a dive during the 200m and injure your knee."

Ali was dumbfounded. "What? No way, man, that's gonna hurt, and what's the point?"

"I only need you to go down and stay down for about two minutes, screaming as loud as you can. This will give me the time I need to get myself over that far wall." Ali slowly nodded as if he was finally understanding his mission. I felt like I was Tom Cruise in a *Mission Impossible* movie. I won't lie, it was exciting!

"Say I do it...what's in it for me?"

Ali was pretty easy to win over, as chips were his weakness. He would do absolutely anything for a bag of chips. I told him I would bring him back a bag, and he was in. Now we were two.

I kept my eyes on the wall. As the 200m race began, Ali took a dive at the first corner, just as we'd discussed. He fell right on schedule. With his first scream of pain, I sprinted to the wall, my heels barely touching the ground. All the staff rushed to their golden goose, and as he yelled, "It hurts!" I threw myself at the wall. I got one leg and then the other over. I was now sitting on the wall, and with a final thrust of both hands, I leapt off and landed flat on my feet on the other side.

When I looked up, I realised that I'd made it. I was out of prison, and not a single person knew I was missing. It felt like that scene from *Shawshank Redemption* when Andy finally escapes the confines of his cell, takes his shirt off, and holds his hands up to the sky. If I had been the hulking beast I am now and not the scrawny kid I was then, I probably would have done the same.

Instead, keeping my shirt on, I started walking to the bus stop, my pace quickening with each step. I was filled with adrenaline, but I knew I wasn't completely free. Not yet. I could still be dragged kicking and screaming back to the school by the headmaster or some wannabe hero of a teacher. In order to complete my escape, I needed to get on the bus to head to the local mall, Whiteleys.

When the bus pulled up, I almost jumped onto it. My mind was filled with excitement and wonder. What would I do in Whiteleys? What would I eat? The food court had a *Pizza Hut*, a popcorn vendor, a candy-floss stand, and so many other mouth-watering options.

The arcade area had all the latest games: *Mortal Kombat 3, San-Francisco: Rush, Virtual-Cop.* You name it, it was there, and each could be played with a single 50p coin. My fingers started to twitch just from the thought of playing those games.

The lazy bus conductor didn't charge me for riding the bus for those ten stops. He probably thought I was under-age (I told you I was scrawny), or he felt bad about charging a kid.

When the bus arrived at Whiteleys in Paddington, I jumped off and ran in. I went straight to the food court. I was famished and parched. I went straight up to the *Pizza Hut* cashier and said I needed a large cheese pizza, a large cola, and cheese bites. As I said each of these items, I think I actually started to salivate. I'm sorry, but I was starving.

The cashier put the order through and asked me how I would be paying. I reached into my pocket for my little wallet and realised my pocket was empty; my wallet was in my trousers and my trousers were at home. Reality hit me. I was in my P.E. kit, in the middle of a shopping centre, with not a single penny on me.

Remember I was telling you about how my mouth started to salivate at the thought of having my own pizza? Well, my mouth started to dry up now as I realised there was nothing I could do, nothing at all. I was starving to the point that I think I was suffering from malnutrition. You're probably wondering, teenage reader of the modern era, why I didn't use something like *Apple Pay*. Well, this was the late 1990s, and *Nokia* brick phones weren't that advanced. They only allowed for calls and SMS text messages. The screen back then wasn't even a colour screen. Instead, it was a sickly green colour, which was perfect: I felt sick to my stomach too. Plus, along with my wallet, my Nokia brick phone was back at home in my school trouser pocket, so I couldn't even call one of my friends for back-up.

As much as I was pushing the thought to the very, very back of my mind, I realised what I had to do: I had to go back to school and face the music. To make matters worse, I would have to WALK back to school as I didn't want to try my bad luck on a bus. I had no way of paying for my journey, and it was actually a criminal offence to fare-evade on purpose. If the bus conductor asked me to pay for the journey, I was done for.

It was a long walk back. When I finally reached the school, I decided I could still try and sneak in; maybe nobody had realised I was gone? Perhaps I could climb back over the wall and reinsert myself into my Form group? No harm, no foul, and nobody had to know about my ill-advised excursion to the mall.

I walked up the main road and stealthily crept through the alley on tiptoes so as not to make any noise. I then knelt down and then jumped onto the wall, like those cats do in those *TikTok* videos.

I landed on the other side and looked up to see the headmaster standing there. I was caught by 'the prison warden' because he'd been waiting for me...and it wasn't just him. The whole school had been waiting for me. I'd learn later that when they called my name for the 400m (what an idiot I was for signing up for that!), and I hadn't come forward, the P.E. teachers quickly realised I was off-site because I'd been marked as present during morning registration. As it was a safety issue, the headmaster had been notified, and so here we all were.

'The warden' put his hand on my shoulder, telling me quite bluntly, "You have a lot of explaining to do." He marched me to his office in silence, and it was in that office that I learnt the gravity of what I'd done.

My mum was sitting outside the head's office, her face buried in her hands. "Mrs Ullah, we've found him," the head bellowed across the corridor, and my poor little mum looked up. Her eyes were red and bloodshot. She'd been crying, and this immediately shattered my heart into a million pieces. She was so overcome that she could barely speak and managed to whisper, "Where were you?" I had nothing. No smart reply and no excuse. I'd upset my mother, and this was completely inexcusable.

The meeting that followed was not a pleasant one, trust me. The headmaster told me that when a child goes missing, the policy is to immediately inform parents in accordance with the school's safeguarding regulations. I imagined my mum getting that phone call telling her that one of her sons had gone missing, and I almost cried just at the thought of it. I'd been so fixated on my 'prison break' that I'd not for one second given any thought to the ramifications of my actions and how they might play out in the real world.

I was excluded for a week and grounded at home for two weeks. In the end, I really did complete a prison sentence, and this time, there was no escape.

Take what you want from this episode, dear reader, but the lesson I took from it was a simple but powerful one: think your actions through, and look at every decision you make from every angle possible, going from the best-case to the worst-case scenario. Sometimes, your imagination may get the best of you, and I wish I had considered my 'prison break' from the perspective of the head (who received the news that a child in his school had gone missing), the school receptionist (who had to make a difficult phone call) and my mother (who had to hear over the phone that one of her sons was nowhere to be found). While I was standing in Whiteleys ordering a pizza, so many adults, including my own mother, were in a state of panic because I decided I was too good for the school food on Sports Day.

Chapter Eight
STRANGER DANGER!

Before mobile phones had 4K cameras (and before your phone was basically a supercomputer in the palm of your hand), any budding videographer needed a digital camcorder to be able to film anything. You also needed a laptop computer to do anything PC related on the go. In the early 2000s, both of these were quite expensive for your average teenager.

So, dear reader, when my elder brother and I were returning a film to the now non-existent *Blockbuster* video store on a cold Saturday morning in December, it should not surprise you that we were quite excited by the Irishman with a beard the colour of a tangerine who offered both of these at a very affordable price when he pulled up next to us in his red *Volkswagen*. Seeing as he came bearing gifts in December, let's call him 'Ginger Santa'. My eyes lit up as I eyed the silver *Sony Handycam* he offered for £50, while my brother was gravitating towards the *Sony* laptop, which was being offered for £150. I think he was thinking that buying it would mean he would be able to do his school homework on it rather than on the family computer. Bear in mind, back then, the camera would have been about £300, and the laptop would easily be around £600. Both seemed to be brand new and were housed in a small, brown duffel bag. They seemed <u>completely</u> legit.

Being teenagers, we did not exactly walk around with that kind of money, and the kind 'Ginger Santa' offered to walk us to the ATM so my brother could withdraw the cash. I remember that he seemed to smile a lot (the way that a Santa impressionist does at a retail store) as my brother withdrew £200 from his student savings account at *Barclays Bank*.

'Ginger Santa' walked us back to his red *Volkswagen* sleigh, and we were all set for the exchange: a brand new Sony camcorder with a reversible screen and a Sony laptop for £200 of cold, hard cash.

The next part happened in slow motion (or at least it plays back in slow-motion in my mind whenever I try to remember it). This is how it went down: I kept my eyes on the laptop and camcorder as 'Ginger Santa' showed them to us once more before putting them back into the brown duffel bag beside him. I did not want to blink as I felt somewhere deep in the pit of my stomach that we were about to be scammed. However, I trusted my brother, and I thought he would have caught on by this point if it WAS some kind of scam. I reassured myself that this was simply 'Ginger Santa' selling off some old items to kids in the street. I remember keeping my eyes open so hard that small tears had started to form in the corners of my eyes, the way they do when you enter into a staring-contest with your frenemy at school. I saw 'Ginger Santa' put both items into the bag, reach down to pick it up from beside him and hand my brother the bag as he simultaneously took the cash from him.

"Thanks lads," was all I remember him saying as he came out of slow-motion, turned on the car's ignition and sped off down St John's Wood. I urged my brother to let me see the camera so I could try it out, but he refused, telling me that it could be dangerous as there may be crooks around. This was true: we were, after all, two teenagers holding very expensive items in the middle of London at the dodgy end of St John's Wood.

We scuttled into our house and then into my brother's room, giddy with excitement. I could not wait to try out the camcorder, and my brother was saying something about doing his homework on the go. As I closed his bedroom door and turned to walk back towards his bed, where he was sitting with the bag open, I heard my brother's primal scream and then the word, "No!" This echoed throughout the entire bedroom and still rings in my ears to this day when I recall the event. "It can't be," I thought. What could possibly have gone wrong? Why was my brother screaming, and in what way could we have been ripped off and scammed? These were questions that flooded my mind, finally breaking through the cage of reassurance I had placed them in.

When I turned the corner of the bedroom, I saw my brother, his face red with anger, worry, and fear, holding the two items in his hands. Was it the *Sony Handycam* and laptop, I hear you ask, dear reader? The answer is of course, "no!" Instead, my brother was holding in his hands (which were trembling so much he was about to drop them) two medium-sized bottles of *Evian* water, both filled to the top with sand.

In the aftermath, during the family meeting at which we were both grounded for two weeks, we concluded that we had both been duped (of course) at a professional level by a professional con-artist.

Now, at this point, you might be wondering, "well, what happened?" After much deliberation and dramatically re-enacting the event, I can tell you this much: there HAD been a camcorder and a laptop, both were indeed working, and both had been placed in the duffel bag. The problem was that there had actually been TWO duffel bags. We were handed a replica duffel bag which was the same size, shape, and colour as the one the laptop and camera had been placed in, except our one housed two bottles of *Evian* filled with sand (to give it the necessary weight) for which we had gladly paid £200.

You can decide, dear reader, at what point, if any, you would have turned away. Perhaps if you had been in my *Nike Air* shoes back then, you may have acted differently. Maybe you would have insisted he step out of his red Volkswagen when he handed you the duffel bag containing the goods. Or, quite possibly, you would have simply told 'Ginger Santa' "No, thank you" when he offered the laptop and camcorder at such cheap prices in the middle of the streets. For me, the lesson I learnt that day when I saw my brother holding the world's most expensive *Evian* bottles is that if a deal seems too good to be true, it probably is.

Chapter Nine

NEVER BACK DOWN!

At the beginning of Year Ten, just as the new term started, my family moved me to a new school. "It's for your own good," they said. Apparently, my current school, London Community School, where I'd spent Years Seven to Nine, turned foul in Year Ten for students. Senior years at LCS were completed in a different building, and it was rumoured that at the upper school, students smoked cigarettes in the toilets at break time, among other things. There may even have been some truth in it, and this is rooted in the fact that not long after I left, the school was permanently shut down and turned into an academy.

My parents did not want their beloved son to be exposed to the acts of immorality that those upper school students were involved in and, therefore, moved me to Victoria Academy on Buckingham Palace Road. "It's right beside the Queen's house," my father told me in a reassuring tone – as if Her Majesty would come to my rescue if I was being bullied or beaten up.

I arrived at the new school on September 6th at 8:30 a.m. Almost immediately, I felt like an outsider. In the corridors, as the headmaster walked me to my Form class, 10B, I noticed that kids were huddled together in groups. This was no surprise – they'd known each other a number of years, and all the friendship groups had already been decided. I was the outsider.

The headmaster dropped me off at the door. "Have a good day, young sir," was all he said before walking off. There was going to be nothing 'good' about this first day. I was sure of it. I, therefore, expected the worst.

When I entered the classroom, my first thought was to sit down, dip low into my chair, and vanish into obscurity until the first lesson. The problem was that all the tables and chairs were taken either by a pair of students and a desk or by one student taking up a whole set of desks, even using one as a footstool. Some students even stood and leaned on the wall in order to speak to their friends.

The only tables that were free were the four tables right in the middle of the room. This nest had three chairs, and nobody was sitting on any of them. "Well, that's weird," I thought, concluding that maybe these three students were absent. This meant that, at least for now, I could sit down.

As soon as I did, everyone let out a gasp and then an "Oooh..." Even the form tutor, Mr Rockwell, stopped mid-register when he saw me slide into the forsaken chair. I did not get what the big deal was, but in stunned silence, everyone just stared at the classroom door. They seemed to be waiting for something or someone.

I had no idea what to expect until 'Mike Tyson' walked through the door. I am not exaggerating. Hand on heart, this 'teenager' in Year Ten literally looked like the former heavyweight champion, complete with the stone-cold stare, military-style haircut, and closely shaven goatee. He even had his chin tucked in, the way that Tyson always had during his entrances, and there were a pair of boxing gloves hanging around his neck as if he had just come from a fight.

This was Tyrone. I'd later learn that Tyrone had failed Year Eleven and was, therefore, repeating his GCSEs a second time. He was basically an eighteen-year-old and legally an adult. This was no surprise because, trust me, he LOOKED it.

Tyrone came into the classroom and stopped dead in his tracks when he saw me sitting at his desk. "Oh dear", I hear you saying, dear teenage reader...oh dear, indeed. My heart sank to the pit of my stomach, and I felt sick with anxiety to the point I wanted to throw up. It suddenly dawned on me why this small island of tables, along with four chairs, was left untouched. It was reserved specifically for 'Iron Mike'.

Without saying anything, I shot Mr Rockwell a desperate look, begging for his intervention. Mr Rockwell gave me a look right back, and I could read his reply in his face: "Don't look at me. You got yourself into this." He then looked back down at his register, ignoring my inevitable showdown with 'Mike Tyson'. Thanks, Mr Rockwell, thanks a lot.

'Iron Mike' walked right up to me, and everyone just held their breath. He SLAMMED him his bare-knuckle fists on the desk. I could see my terrified reflection in his eyes, but I did not want to back down. In that frenzied millisecond, when I looked at him and he at me, I realised that being new was one of those moments which would shape how my classmates saw me. "I won't give into fear because I'm not a coward," I thought to myself. So I just sat there, refusing to get up. What I did do, though, was try to distract myself. Now, I don't know about you, but in tense moments like this, I like to cast my mind back to more calming moments in my life or recall a fact that could calm me down. Unfortunately, on this occasion, all my brain did was recall a fact I'd seen on a *Channel 4* documentary one time, which was that on July 26th, 1986, Mike Tyson knocked out Marvis Frazier in thirty seconds. Thanks, brain. You and Mr Rockwell should meet as you have both been equally useless to me on this occasion.

I braced myself for my very own thirty-second knockout...but it never came. 'Tyson' just said, "You're new, innit? Boy, you're brave, cuz, but it's cool."

He pulled out one of the remaining chairs and sat down. The entire class (including Mr Rockwell) breathed sighs of relief, and I thanked God that I hadn't been floored by 'the Champ' on my first day.

Now, you're probably wondering what the lesson is in all of this, and I'm not really sure what to tell you. They say that ignorance is bliss, but on this occasion, that bliss lasted about half a second as I was quickly confronted with the very real possibility of being pummelled to death in front of a teacher who would probably do nothing about it. I did win the respect of the class after this, though, and in all my years, I never once fell out or got into a fight with someone in my Form. In my own stoic way, my refusal to back down or get up meant that I'd stood my ground against the biggest guy in the year group and held my own. I mean, I'd held my own because I was like a deer caught in the headlights, too terrified to move an inch from my chair, but I did stay put, and that's all anyone saw.

Perhaps then, teenage reader, the lesson here is to stand up for yourself when you need to and show courage in the face of adversity. This could be when facing an exam that you feel you should have revised for, telling a friend who made an unkind joke that it wasn't very nice or telling 'Mike Tyson' to find his own chair.

Chapter Ten

DON'T TRUST THE BARBERS

Have you ever needed a haircut SO badly? You know? When your hair grows out to the point that you look like a homeless person or someone who has yet to discover a pair of scissors? I implore you, dear teenage reader, when you do find yourself in such a position, do not ever do what I did that time in Year Ten. It may just get you in serious trouble.

It was October, my second month in a new school. The autumn leaves were falling from the trees, and everyone was bracing themselves for the new season with new threads, new kicks, and classy trims. Everyone, that is, except me. I'd spent the summer growing out my hair for a very good cause: I was racing my elder brother, who told me he would pay me £50 if I managed to get its length, from root to tip, to 50cm by October. I planned to use that money to buy myself the new *Nike* trainers.

As I was new to this school, I used the first non-uniform day to proudly walk into school with my new trainers, telling everyone how I'd won the bet. The problem was that nobody cared about the bet or the trainers. Everyone kept saying that my hair made me look like Albert Einstein's great grandfather. "Bruv, I ain't gonna lie, it looks like you've got a bird's nest on your head," commented my new friend Ibrahim, with my other friend Fazlu concurring. By break time, the abuse got so bad that even the teachers had started to join in: "Shampoo was invented in the 16th century..." my history teacher Mr Williams quipped, winking at me as he did. "So what?" I thought. "At least I've GOT hair, unlike you. Your hairline is so high it looks like it's trying to run away from your forehead!"

By period four, I made up my mind that I was going to use my lunch money to pop out of school and get a haircut, popping back well before the beginning of period five. As soon as the bell rang for the one-hour lunch break, I headed for the gates. *Luigi's*, the local Italian barbershop, was ten minutes down the road near Pimlico. That gave me forty minutes to have my haircut before I had to head back to school. "I'm gonna make it," I thought.

I'd been cutting my hair at *Luigi's* for a while now, and I knew all the barbers there. There was Luigi himself, an elderly gentleman named Menos, and Rick. Menos always liked to remind me how I used to cry like a baby when I first got there because he would straighten the back of my hair, cutting off the poor excuse of a ponytail that used to grow at the back of my head.

It was indeed Menos who was free when I walked in that afternoon, which was great: he knew how my hair grew, and he knew just the way to cut it so that the sides didn't stick up, making me look like *Sonic the Hedgehog*.

"Yo, where you been hidin'? Too big for us to cut your hair now?" Menos asked.

"Nah, man, I've been growing it out like *Rambo*, but now it's too long."

Menos nodded, sitting me down and putting wet fingers through my hair. "Okay then, let's get you sorted out, but it looks like it's gonna take a while. What the bloody hell you got growing in here, an ant farm? I'm gonna give you a wash and a fresh cut, don't worry."

Then, without warning, Menos sprayed my head with the shower hose, immediately squishing blue shampoo out of the transparent bottle. He jerked my head back and started rinsing it out while adding more of that silky shampoo onto my head.

The next part I take full responsibility for. Full responsibility. Maybe it was the warm water on my head, the scalp massage involved in the washing of my caveman-style hair, or just the effect of the aromatic lavender fragrance emanating from the shampoo itself. Whatever it was, all I know is that it put me to sleep. A deep sleep.

When I awoke, fifty-five minutes had passed, and my class was well into period five. At first, I wasn't exactly sure where I was. Then reality hit me like a tonne of bricks. Menos was just trimming the edges of my sideburns when I almost jumped out of the chair. He held up the mirror against the back of my head so I could see in the mirror I was facing just how finely he had cut it. "Almost done, my friend, looking SLICK! A nice new trim for you." Menos was admiring his handiwork, the way in which an artist admires his painting. I almost screamed at him.

"Menos, you know I have to be in SCHOOL, right?!"

"What? I thought it was one of those early finishes today..."

I didn't let him finish. I threw myself off the chair, dashed the money in his hand and raced out the door.

There were tiny strands of hair on my face, but I didn't care. I bolted down the road. I meandered through at least ten mums pushing baby buggies, two Onyx public cleaners, three people in wheelchairs, and a Japanese tourist group taking pictures with a public phone booth. I know it's London, but why was it so busy today of all days? I had to literally jump through the gaps I saw so that I didn't flatten anybody.

When I finally reached the school gates, I sprinted the last hurdle to my classroom. I was dishevelled, sweating, and panting for my life, but I MADE it to catch the last bit of period five. Perhaps it was the adrenaline in my blood, but I honestly thought I deserved a cheer when I opened the door to the classroom. Nobody cheered, though. Instead, I received a cold reception from my fellow students and my teacher, Señorita Martinez (she insisted on the 'Señorita'). I was late to Spanish.

Now, it's pretty terrible to be twenty-five minutes late to ANY teacher's class, but you only arrive twenty-five minutes late to Señorita Martinez if you have a death wish. She can speak fluent English, but when she's angry, she goes into full-on, quick-fire Spanish as if she were a character in an R-rated Spanish film, except there aren't any subtitles. You're left wondering if she's gonna pull out a machete and slice you in half right there like some raging, psychotic Salma Hayek. 'Psycho Hayek's' hair would stand up too when she yelled as if she was being put through electric shock treatment. That's how much her blood boiled when a student was late.

Well, her rant started with "Estas loca?!" I was able to mentally translate this to, "Are you crazy?" This was thanks to singer Ricky Martin and his song, *Livin La Vida Loca*. What followed this psychotically-infused rhetorical question is beyond me, and I pretty much zoned out during her Spanish tirade. There was a lot of screaming and plenty of frenzied hand gestures. The only other word I DID understand was the last word because it roughly sounded the same in English: "Una hora detención." I had a one-hour detention with 'Psycho Hayek' the next day, or "Meñana" as she liked to call it.

Of course, she phoned my parents to notify them twenty-four hours before (because that's the school policy), so I got another earful when I reached home, too. It wouldn't be the first time, trust me.

I can't exactly blame 'Psycho Hayek' for her reaction, though. I mean, her rage was a bit extreme, but I was twenty-five minutes late to a forty-five-minute lesson. Nobody, not Señorita Martinez, not my Head of Year, and not even my family wanted to hear my side of the story – that I had innocently fallen asleep during a carefully thought-out, well-planned trip to the barbers. So, teenage reader, my advice to you from this episode is always to factor in things going wrong during any kind of trip. Factor in traffic (even if it is human traffic of old people and babies in prams) and always factor in the fact that the human body is frail, and at any given point, you may just rest your head only to find that you have fallen asleep at a critical moment when you absolutely should not be asleep.

Chapter Eleven

MIND THAT BUS

Being the wonderful teenage reader that you are, you know more than anyone that as well-meaning and earnest as your younger siblings may be, sometimes they are just downright annoying. I say with deliberate intent that on occasion, there are moments when you just want to drive them to an orphanage and leave them there with a sign hanging around their neck that reads, "Feed me." What I will preamble this episode with, though, is that if and when they do request a bit of your food or a sip of one of your fizzy drinks, just GIVE it to them and don't do what I did. I speak from experience in this regard because on one such occasion, when my youngest baby brother wanted a sip of my cola, I refused to give him some, and it almost cost me my life.

Being in Year Ten at the time, I felt like a whole new man when I turned fifteen that year, and I believed it was important that a man had an occasional drink of cola from one of those oversized cups that you get at the cinema.

Thus, on one fateful afternoon in January, a few days after my birthday, I was heading home from school, pleased to be alive. I'd been praised by my English teacher for an answer I'd given in class, and I was feeling pretty good about myself. Pretty darn good. I, therefore, decided I should reward myself with a huge cup of cola, which I would sip on my way home. Nothing beats the satisfying feeling of drinking an ice-cold cola after a long day at school. Getting off the bus early, I bought it from *Blue Shop* next to my house. *Blue Shop* sold it in one of those big plastic cups that seem to have no bottom.

When I reached home, I was still casually sipping the large cola, and there was still about half of the drink left in the huge cup. "Fine," I thought, "I'll have the rest of it with my dinner." When my mother opened the door, though, my little baby brother saw me holding the cola cup and immediately demanded that I give it to him. Now, to this day, I still regret my actions following this request because it was mean-spirited, but also because it almost cost me my life. I told him, "Go get your own, you little crybaby." Being aged three, he started crying, and he was crying profusely. Non-stop.

This caught my mother's attention. "You see what you did? Now give him that stupid cup of cola, and be done with it." Back then, I was quite stubborn, and I did NOT want to concede to my baby brother; he might consider it a weakness, and it could become something he could exploit when the stakes were higher, such as those rare occasions I secretly bought a vanilla ice-cream from the ice-cream truck. What if he saw me on one of those days I would sneak out and buy myself one and demand that I hand it over through those same crocodile tears? I couldn't risk it. I told my mother, "Mum, It's mine, and if he wants one, he can just grow up and buy himself one like I did!" Not my proudest moment as an elder brother, I know. With that, I went to my room, slammed the door shut on his teary face, put my headphones on, and turned on my *Sony Walkman* cassette to listen to *The Backstreet Boys*.

It was not until that same time the next day, after school, that my baby brother's teary face flashed before my mind's eye. "Poor kid", I thought to myself. I'd shown him something new and shiny, dangled it in front of him, and then told him he couldn't have it. To rectify the situation, I decided I would once again get off the bus early to cross the road to *Blue Shop* and buy him that same large cup of cola.

When the bus stopped at Edgware Road, I got off and walked around the front of the bus to cross the road as *Blue Shop* was on the other side. Big mistake! Edgware Road has two lanes of traffic on either side and the bus, for me, produced a blind spot. I did not see the other bus until it was too late. It had gone around my bus, and it hit me from the side. It sent me flying into the air before stopping immediately. I fell to the side of the road. Seemingly unhurt, I immediately got up and was standing on both feet when a terrible thought occurred to me: am I dead? In all the films I'd seen (such as *Ghost* starring the late Patrick Swayze), when a person dies, they step out of their body, the ghost wearing the same clothes they were wearing when they died. I froze in fear, as I was, of course, still wearing the same clothes and appeared totally unhurt. Did I dare turn around to look at the ground? I was afraid that I would see my dead corpse. I summoned up all my courage and counted to five. On the count of five, I turned around and was relieved to see the gritty, grey road. No dead replica.

At that point, the bus driver – an elderly man in his fifties – popped his head out of the driver's window. He had, after all, just hit a kid as a London bus driver, and he needed to soothe his guilty conscience. "You alright, mate? Here, how many fingers am I holding up?" When I confirmed that he was indeed holding up three fingers, he responded with, "Good enough for me, mate," and drove off. Nice. No guilty conscience or criminal record. I still ride the buses in London, but the number thirty-six bus still sends shivers all over my body.

I then noticed that my leg was hurting quite a bit, and when I rolled up my trousers, I saw that my shin was acutely bleeding. However, that was the extent of my injuries. It was a small miracle that I had been hit (well, nudged) by a bus on one of London's main roads, and I was able to walk away mostly unharmed. I did go to *Blue Shop* and got my brother that cold beverage, which had been the root of all the trouble. I told myself that the whole ordeal was a valuable lesson that I had learnt in hindsight: if your little brother wants some of your cola, for heaven's sake, just give it to him.

Chapter Twelve
STOP, IN THE NAME OF THE LAW!

I wanted to be a policeman ever since I saw *The X Files* on television when I was eleven years old, with Mulder and Scully kicking down a criminal's door and yelling, "FEDERAL AGENTS! Show me your hands!" It gave me such a buzz watching that show, and as I entered my teenage years, this desire solidified to the extent that I didn't just want to be a policeman in uniform. No. I wanted to be a detective, or even better, an undercover officer involved in those sting operations where you infiltrate the criminal underworld in order to crack it open from the inside. I wanted to be injured (not mortally, maybe just a shoulder wound) during the final showdown, and I wanted the subsequent ceremony, where I would be awarded a special medal for bravery in front of all my fellow officers and the media, of course. Yes, dear teenage reader. I wanted it all, just like in the films. In a strange kind of way, I got my wish one April when I was in Year Ten, so I thought I'd share that story with you.

I was heading home after school, walking towards that dreaded sixteen bus from Victoria back to Edgware Road. As I've already mentioned, having joined in September, I'd made some friends by April, and these were little

Ibrahim and Fazlu, alongside some others. The three of us were walking towards the bus stop on Buckingham Palace Road, talking about the latest game on *PlayStation, Crash Bandicoot 3: The Wrath Of Cortex*. It's an adventure game where you have to escape various traps in order to reach the end. You've probably played the HD remake of that old classic.

As I was listening to Ibrahim, I noticed in the far right corner of my eye a brutish sort of man being held down by two security guards. I stopped to see what was happening, and my two friends stopped as well. The brute of a man seemed to be trying to push the security guards off, but they had him pinned to the floor, with one of the guards using his knee to hold the hulking man to the ground. The brute had long, oily hair, was wearing a black vest and dark jeans, and was covered in tattoos. For this reason, I shall henceforth call him 'the Undertaker' for the remainder of this episode. A plain-clothes policeman then came to join the other two, and all three tried to contain the thug while the police car arrived. Suddenly, 'the Undertaker' pushed off all three men, so they went flying onto the pavement. He then RAN down the pavement, fleeing the scene, with the three men picking themselves up and sprinting after him.

The chase was on, and I wasn't going to miss it. No way. I bolted after 'the Undertaker' and three men, giving my friends little choice but to follow. The plain-clothes police officer was yelling into his radio: "Suspect is in a black vest, heading west on Victoria, towards Victoria Station. Suspect was caught stealing in *Boots* Pharmacy."

The chase was now TRULY on. I could hear the police sirens ringing in the distance, and I was living this moment with every ounce of my being: my fists were clenched white, my heart was beating about a billion beats a minute, and my feet were pounding the pavement as I followed the thief, the plain-clothes policeman and the security guards.

'The Undertaker' ran straight into Victoria Underground Station. We lost Fazlu on the way, and Ibrahim, panting, caught up to me and said, through some heavy breathing, "I'm sorry, man, I've only got a bus pass. I can't come." I wanted to tell him that a bus pass was all I had, too, but before I could, he turned and walked off. Ibrahim saw and appreciated his limits.

I, on the other hand, did not. I ran straight into the underground station, keeping behind the plain-clothes officer.

Entering the underground tube station, the policeman walked straight up to the Transport for London (TFL) staff. He flashed his badge and said, in an authoritative tone, a phrase he had probably repeated 1000 times: "Undercover police, let me through." They instantly opened the barrier gate and let him through.

My turn, I thought. I gulped and took out my bus pass. "I have one shot at this, so I better not mess it up," I thought, but the gravity of the situation did hit me: I was a school kid about to involve himself in a high-stakes police chase. What could possibly go wrong, except EVERYTHING? I summoned up all my courage, held my breath, and flashed my bus pass, saying with some degree of feigned authority, "I'm with them!" Without saying a word, the TFL staff let me through!

I was stunned; it had worked! As an esteemed member of the current teenage generation, cynical as you are, you probably think I'm making this all up, but honestly, I couldn't make it up if I tried, which is probably why you haven't seen such an account in any other book you've read.

I was now through the barriers, and the bizarre thing is, the actual undercover police officer was on his radio, telling his colleagues 'the Undertaker' had eluded him: "I've lost the subject, I repeat, LOST the subject. Exit lines blocked. I'm pulling back to check the front entrances." It was at this point that I actually believed my own lie and assumed the role of a police officer on the hunt for a shoplifter. There was a chance I could be the one that caught 'the Undertaker'!

Standing there on the platform, I made up my mind. I would help the police catch 'the Undertaker', sustaining some kind of minor injury in the process. I would be given a special Metropolitan Police Bravery Award, and my picture would be published in *The Sun* and *The Guardian* newspapers. Yes, dear teenage reader, I had the PR for this all planned out in my head.

What I did not expect was that while I was walking around the train platforms, I would actually come face-to-face with 'the Undertaker' himself. Fantasy had turned into reality for me, and it was terrifying, let me tell you. We were on the Circle Line. He was standing on the westbound platform, and I was eastbound with No Man's Land between us. I knew that at any point, he could rush towards me and push me onto the electric train lines behind me, resulting in my instant death.

There was utter silence, like in that scene in *The Matrix* when Neo was facing Agent Smith in the underground. The only difference was, of course, that I was not Neo, and this was real life, not a Hollywood movie. "But this was always your dream," I hear you cry. You're right, and up to this point, it HAD BEEN. However, when I found myself faced with an actual criminal in a life-or-death situation, reality hit me, and I regretted chasing a criminal down into the underground tube station.

"Say something...anything", I told myself – and I was shocked by what came out. "Give it up. Crime doesn't pay, so turn yourself in!" Cringe-fest, I know. It was the cheesiest line to ever be uttered by a school student facing a thief, and looking back now, I wish I'd said something cooler. 'The Undertaker's' response was brutal: "You stupid little kid, you got some kind of death wish?" I honestly don't blame him for saying what he did. I mean, look at the situation: I was a scrawny teenager telling him, a hulking beast of a man who had thrown off a whole bunch of security guards, to turn himself in.

The next moment is one I replay again and again in my mind in slow motion in order to relish it because it was probably one of the coolest moments in my whole teenage life.

This is how it goes down. The train arrives at the platform behind 'the Undertaker'. He turns and runs onto it. I see the undercover officer in the corner, unaware of this and still searching for his suspect. He is within earshot of me, and I, therefore, scream, in my best teenager-that-thinks-he-is-a-policeman voice, "He's on the Circle Line westbound train, all units, GO, GO, GO!" A wave of officers then FLOOD the Circle Line platforms, and IT IS GLORIOUS. They try to pry the doors open, but to no avail, and as the train starts moving, the undercover officer screams into his radio: "Suspect spotted getting onto the westbound Circle Line train, apprehend him at Sloane Square station."

I remember standing there, just in awe at the number of officers on the platform that I had summoned. "I did that," I told myself. That was all me. I felt a hand on my shoulder and looked up to see it was the plain-clothes policeman. A simple "thanks" was all I got before he walked off. No Metropolitan Bravery Award. No ceremony. No puff piece in the newspaper. I was so disappointed. I felt so let down by the police after I'd risked my life to catch a criminal for them.

It was while I was lying in bed that evening, playing back the events of that afternoon, that I realised why I'd felt so disappointed. In my mind, I'd lived a part of something I'd dreamt of since I was a kid, and the reality was that I would never live up to those lofty expectations. Life rarely does, but it can surprise you in other ways. While I always dreamt of being a police officer when I grew up, I never thought that as a teenager, I'd have a hand in actually apprehending a real-life thief, one that was a spitting image of a WWE wrestler. That may well just be your little takeaway from this episode: never expect life to live up to your dreams, but do expect life to throw surprises your way that you never, ever dreamt of.

Chapter Thirteen

NEVER EXPECT APOLOGIES

I must have been at the ripe old age of fifteen when I hit that forty-year-old man with an umbrella on a rainy day on the back of his head, and let me tell you, I still chuckle when I remember it. In my defence, at the moment of impact, I was (in my mind at least) totally justified, but I'm getting ahead of myself. Let me start at the beginning.

I was in Year Ten at the time, and it was May. I was settling into my new school, and this process was about as comfortable as going to the toilet to do a number two in your best friend's house; you hope it doesn't smell too bad, and honestly, you just hope for the best.

A significant portion of the academic year had passed, but I had yet to make a good impression on my classmates. In Year Ten, proving your masculinity really matters. A LOT. It's a bit like being in prison – you need to avoid making enemies but also show everyone that you're not one to be messed with. Acting too much like a 'rude boy' means the subject teachers hate you, and acting too much like a geek means you get your lunch money taken off you on a daily basis by kids in Year Seven. It's all about treading a fine balance, and I had not done anything to place myself directly between these two extremes.

A rare opportunity to prove myself presented itself on a rainy day after school as I was heading towards Victoria bus station with my classmates.

I mentioned it was raining, right? It had been so since the morning, and I'd therefore packed my £1 mini umbrella in my bag. It was one of those cheap ones that extended like a Japanese Bo stick, which I always thought was quite cool.

Everyone was carrying umbrellas that evening at 4 p.m., including a 'Blonde Barbie' on her way home from work. I remember this huge head of hair that looked salon-ready. She had a huge umbrella, which she was using to keep the product (conditioner and God knows what else) intact. As I walked past her, Barbie's umbrella clipped my ear. I don't know if you've ever been flicked on the ear, but when it's raining and the cold chill of the wind is biting into your skin like a thousand knives, it hurts. A lot. I turned around to see if the woman was going to apologise, but instead, I saw a greying man in a suit, who seemed to be approaching his forties, laughing his head off. Let's call this man 'George Clooney'.

I was already livid, my blood boiling over with anger, and when I saw 'Clooney' laughing at me, I absolutely lost it. "How dare he?" I thought. Doesn't he know that it feels as if someone has just pierced your ear in the middle of Antarctica when your ear is clipped by an umbrella the way mine was? Well, let's see how he likes it, was the logical conclusion I came to. Now, granted, I should have perhaps gone over and at least had a conversation with him before I did what I did, but I was a teenager, and we teens are NOT to be messed with, especially in the rain. As a side note, I was also in the presence of my classmates, and I wanted to prove to them that I wasn't going to take his laughing at me lying down, especially as I was armed with an ancient samurai weapon of sorts. I extended my Japanese Bo stick of an umbrella, walked over to him, and, as he was walking away, clipped him purposefully on the ear.

He stopped dead in his tracks. My heart skipped about ten beats as he turned around, grabbed me by my collar (a constant re-occurrence for me, it seems), lifted me off my feet, and pinned me against the nearest wall. I was now at eye level with 'Clooney', and let me tell you, this lookalike had none of the charisma Clooney does in the films. "You stupid kid, what's wrong with you?"

I could barely speak, but I managed to let out, "Yeah...how'd you like it?"

"What?!"

I responded, slowly gaining my confidence, "I saw you laughing when that woman's umbrella hit me, so how'd you like it?"

"I wasn't laughing at you, you idiot. I was laughing at the woman because she should have apologised to you but didn't."

"Oh dear," I thought. Oh dear indeed. I literally had nothing left to say and was dumbfounded. I'd assumed he was laughing at me and had acted on that assumption. Looking back now, this was very foolish, but I had to stand my ground. "You're lying" was all I could come up with, and it did not go down well, trust me. He pressed on my chest even harder now so that I could barely breathe, and he had this crazy look in his eyes. I could see the red veins in his eyes, which looked like they were about to pop. I was the instigator of this entire situation, and it was quickly spiralling way out of control. His other hand was still by his side, and I noticed he was beginning to clench it into a solid fist.

Fortunately, my classmates came to my rescue by threatening him. My little friend Ibrahim found the confidence to remind 'Clooney' of the facts of the situation, saying, "Do summink, bruv, what you gonna do, hit a kid? There are cameras on this road, and we're all witnesses." The man's eyes darted left and right, and he realised he could very well be arrested for the assault of a minor if he did inflict any actual damage on a teenager. While all of this was going on, I was mentally preparing myself for him to choke-slam me onto the pavement.

Instead, much to my relief, 'Clooney' put me down, let out a groan of exasperation, and walked away, heading towards Victoria tube station. My friends huddled towards me, and we began to whisper and laugh about the situation. We'd collectively faced off against a grown man and won. I started to feel a sense of camaraderie and belonging with the group, as I truly felt they had come to my rescue in a real-world situation outside of school.

As I was filled with these feelings of brotherhood, I found that my fear drained away. Well, almost. Just as the panic, anxiety, and fear were all leaving my body, they returned immediately when I saw the man marching (yes, marching) towards me with a clear intent and purpose.

"Oh dear," I thought. "I'm dead meat. He's obviously changed his mind and is returning to knock me out", I thought to myself. To make matters worse, when my new 'brothers-in-arms' saw him coming, they shuffled away from me so that I was left standing on the pavement on my own. They offered me to him like some sacrificial lamb being offered to a lion by the others. Eat him, not us.

I closed my eyes and braced for impact, but nothing happened. Well, nothing happened to ME. I felt my hand jerk and instinctively opened my eyes. I noticed that 'Clooney' had grabbed my umbrella from my hand. He lifted it above his head, extended it into a Japanese Bo stick the way that I had, and brought it down on his knee, snapping the metal part in half.

He put the two pieces back in my hand, gave a kind of strange nod, and walked off without saying a word.

I was literally dumbstruck. I realised I had been holding my breath since I'd seen him marching back and had held my breath throughout his execution of my umbrella. I exhaled hard and stood there a minute, processing all that had happened. "That was mad, bruv," Ibrahim finally exclaimed, breaking the silence.

"Yeah, man, let's get home before we get into any more fights with random people," was all I could muster in terms of a reply.

On the way home, I laughed to myself about all that had transpired. I'd been hit on the ear, hit another man on his ear, and then had my umbrella broken into two by that same man. In all seriousness, it could have gotten worse, and may well have, if it hadn't occurred in a public place involving teenagers in school uniform.

Reflecting back on it now, I realise it was my fault, all of it. Turning back to expect a woman who may not have even realised she had clipped me to apologise? My fault. Hitting an absolutely random stranger on the ear? Also my fault. However, my biggest mistake that day was assuming the man's intention for laughing. Seeing red, I had automatically assumed he was laughing at me, when in actual fact, 'Clooney' was laughing at the woman who clipped a teen and failed to apologise. This assumption was what led me then to, in my mind, retaliate and, in 'Clooney's' mind, attack him without provocation. The lesson I learnt that day? Get all the facts straight through a conversation before using your umbrella as a weapon and attacking an unsuspecting Clooney lookalike, and NEVER expect apologies.

Chapter Fourteen

PICK YOUR BATTLES

Life will put you face-to-face with many a moral dilemma, dear teenage reader, and there may be times when you have mere seconds to make a decision using your moral compass, judging between what's right and wrong, before you have to act or react. The decisions you make in those life-defining moments will stay with you forever and will shape you into the person you grow up to be. I was faced with one such decision in Year Ten during a school fight, and let me tell you, it could have gone either way.

It was May, but it was freezing cold. That's British weather for you. You know when your school is so cheap that they pretend the radiators don't work, and somehow, through some small miracle, they work in the staffroom? Well, when it's that cold, anything and everything irritates you, including an eraser being thrown at your head in the middle of a lesson.

My short little friend Ibrahim had a short little temper, and for the entire science lesson, Hamdan, this naughty kid in the classroom, was throwing tiny bits of an eraser onto him. I should add that Hamdan was biting these pieces off one of those student eraser pencils they sold in the local stationery shop.

I watched Ibrahim flinch every time the small, chewed-off piece of rubber hit his head, and at the 10th piece, Ibrahim finally stood up. He was shaking with rage. "What do you think you're PLAYING at, bruv?" Ibrahim exclaimed. Without warning, he then lunged himself at Hamdan.

At this point in the episode, I need to add that I had a bit of a chequered history with Hamdan, one which dated back to the first day of term. In September, we were both new to the school, and this meant we had to be assigned GCSE classes. I was given the last slot in the ICT class, and Hamdan, who also wanted to do ICT, was forced to take Geography.

Needless to say, he was not a happy bunny, and I had my first school fight with Hamdan over this. Following this fight, Hamdan and I had two more short altercations, and even the teachers knew to keep us away from each other. In a strange kind of way, I guess you could say he was my arch-enemy at school (and we all need one of those).

So, when Ibrahim jumped on Hamdan, Miss Dhar, the science teacher, yelled at us, "Somebody do something and stop them! You know I can't do anything!" She had a point. Standing at four foot five inches, Miss Dhar was a tiny little thing, and if she had tried to stop the fight, she would have gone flying onto the wall and stuck on it like a piece of wet salami.

As I approached the two boys, a strange and somewhat dark thought crossed my mind. Here was my close friend, Ibrahim, in a fight with my arch-enemy, and I had the opportunity to sneak in a few punches before I pulled the two boys apart. The temptation was strong, let me tell you. The more I tried to repress it, the stronger it got, forcing me to decide if I was going to act on it. I almost did. In fact, the only thing that stopped me was the realisation that it would be cowardly and I wouldn't be able to look at myself in the mirror the next morning. This wasn't my fight. While the enemy of my friend is still my enemy, Hamdan hadn't picked a fight with me that morning, and it wasn't morally or ethically right to jump in and give Ibrahim that WWE-style assist (or even to sneak in a few blows).

I must add that all these mental conversations I had with myself happened in the span of a few seconds. By the time I'd concluded I would not provide an assist, Ibrahim had managed to give Hamdan a bloody nose. "He didn't even need my help after all", I thought. I threw myself in between them and split them apart. I don't remember a lot of the finer details of the fight, but I do remember the look that Hamdan shot my way after I split them up. It was a look of acknowledgement combined with a tiny bit of gratitude. As I told you before, being in that school was like being in prison, and Hamdan knew I could easily have acted differently. I had done the right thing rather than what was easy.

In a school fight, you don't have a manager to throw in the towel like you do in a boxing match. Nine times out of ten, one or even both fighters start the fight to save face, desperately hoping that a do-gooder or even a teacher will stop it within a few seconds. This allows both fighters to walk away with dignity, saying, "Yeah, you're lucky it got stopped, or I would have ended you." While this is the case with most school fights, in this case, Hamdan was actually about to be ended by Ibrahim. Thus, in that look Hamdan gave me, he seemed acutely grateful that I'd stopped it when I did, as he was clearly losing. Two against one would have made things a lot, lot worse for him.

Many years later, despite our dark history, Hamdan would come to me and ask for help with his UCAS university application, and I believe this stemmed from the moment I helped him out of that fight with Ibrahim.

Ibrahim was excluded for two days and had to come back to school with his parents for a meeting with the headmaster. Hamdan ended up with a plaster on his nose for four days. Ibrahim's dad had to take the morning off to come and speak to the headmaster, and because of it, his dad sold his *PlayStation* to *Computer Exchange* as a punishment. Ibrahim ended up digging out his *Sega Saturn* from the bottom of the bed just to have something to play. I mean, damn, his dad really hit him where it hurts for a fight that easily could have been avoided.

Teenage life is full of such altercations, and trust me, I've had my fair share. You have to decide if a fight is your fight or someone else's. As you get older, you get stronger, and your fists harden to the point where you can do some some real damage. As I told Ibrahim when we were playing *Street Fighter: The Movie* on his *Sega Saturn* one afternoon, it wasn't worth it, and that's probably the advice I impart to you, my respected teenage reader. Avoid a fight as much as you can, and definitely avoid a fight or even an argument that isn't yours. Help those in need, even if that person in need is someone that you don't like, because in this world of cynicism and negativity, sometimes it's just good to do the right thing.

Chapter Fifteen

ALWAYS PICK 'TRUTH'

You know, the first time I ever went to the zoo, I was about five years old, and even back then, I literally had NO idea that I was going to the zoo that day. I mean, I am sure the teacher had told us that there was a trip that week, but back then, I was still trying to figure out the differences between my left and right hands, checking if they were exactly of equal length.

It was only when we boarded the school minibus that it dawned upon me that we were leaving school. All the teachers on the bus started forcing us to sing that God-awful song, "We're going to the zoo, zoo, zoo, and you can come too, too, too." The news came as a surprise to me. I was grateful that I'd taken a packed lunch to school that day or that I'd have been one of those kids the monkeys threw their bananas at out of sympathy.

It would be many, many years later when I would be confronted once again with London Zoo, only this time I was a bit older. It was June of that glorious summer between Years Ten and Eleven...you know what I'm talking about, dear reader. That summer when mock exams and GCSEs seemed to loom in the distance. They were close enough to give you anxiety if you thought about it too hard but far enough away to let you relax in that last summer of bliss, which would be followed by GCSE exams, AS-level exams, A-level exams, and then university. Essentially, it was the last real summer you could act like a kid to the full extent of the word.

Imran and Fazlu would accompany me on this trip in a strange sort of way. That afternoon, we were bored out of our heads playing *PlayStation* in Fazlu's house on Warren Street, and we decided to go out to Baker Street for a walk and maybe some chips. Fazlu also grabbed his camcorder, as we'd started getting into filming back then.

When we passed Regents Park, I could hear the birds chirping. The sun was out, people were walking around with sandals, and there was just something in the air. I don't know, but it just FELT like one of those summers when the days have no end, and anything is possible.

As we walked further up Marylebone Road, we decided to play a kind of 'truth-or-dare' on the go. My friend Fazlu dared me to either climb over the long, unending black gate on the left or own up to some embarrassing truth. I chose 'dare.' I know. How DUMB could I be? I had no idea what was on the other side of the gate. No idea whose property it was and whether or not it would be considered trespassing if I did go over the gate.

It really was quite a climb, especially as the spokes at the top were fairly uninviting. I mean, as I delicately went over the gate one leg after the other, I thanked God I decided to wear thick jeans that morning, and that's all I'll say on the matter.

When I landed on the other side, I heard my friends literally scarper as if they were running away. I called after them, "Guys, you're going to meet me on the other side, yeah?" Nothing. Not even a whisper of a reply. I was totally alone in what could be a wealthy person's back garden because I decided to follow through on a dare. I could feel my mouth start to dry up as I remembered the fact that trespassing is a genuine crime. I was also reminded of that poem, *Hide and Seek* by Vernon Scannell, which was part of our GCSE English Literature anthology: *"Yes, here you are. But where are they who sought you?"* I mean, I know I wasn't playing hide-and-seek, but I felt that same sense of abandonment the speaker feels by the end of the poem. That "sickening sense of loss" (which is how my English teacher explained that line of the poem).

The best thing to do, I thought to myself, was to sneak out and PRAY that nobody saw me. I mean, it wasn't exactly an impossibility, I thought. It was the middle of the day, and it was summer, so it was quite likely that the owner of whatever garden I was in was on holiday or out enjoying the sun. This would have been the case, probably, but the problem was that I was not IN anyone's garden. Oh no. I was ACTUALLY in London Zoo – specifically, in the chimpanzee section. That's right, dear teenage reader. I had accidentally climbed into London Zoo, into the monkey enclave.

I was alerted to this by the screech I heard above me and the banana peel that was stuck to the bottom of my shoe. I looked to my left and saw the sign on the wall: *Monkey Valley*. I knew I had to get out as I'd heard monkeys could be quite violent. I tiptoed through the area until I saw the fence which cordoned this area off.

Jumping over the fence, I suddenly found myself in a swarm of tourists, the difference being, of course, that they were all ticket holders while I had snuck in without a ticket. They were headed for the exit, and I followed closely behind them. My heart was thumping in my chest as I was TERRIFIED that I would be caught and imprisoned in the zoo, my punishment being community service as a zoologist for the rest of the summer.

The security guard eyed me up and down as I exited the zoo with the tourists. He eyed me up, but he did not ask to see my ticket. Thank God.

It would be a whole MINUTE until I found myself outside the zoo, and it was only then that I breathed a sigh of relief. I was OUT, and it wasn't soon enough, trust me. I don't know if I broke any actual laws, but it felt like I did. I mean, I didn't KNOWINGLY climb into London Zoo. I'd just done it accidentally. So, that was okay, right?

The irony was that when I did make it out, my friends, who had been the ones who dared me to climb over, were nowhere to be seen at all. I learnt later that they had used the camcorder we took with us to film me climbing into the zoo, and Fazlu narrated, "We just dared him to climb into the zoo, and he's doing it...unaware of what he is even climbing into!"

I ended up walking home alone, thinking of my time with the monkeys and the fact that I'd most likely trespassed in London Zoo. The root of all the trouble was, of course, the fact that I'd risen to the challenge of a dare.

That was my fatal error, and it almost cost me my freedom; while teenagers don't go to prison in London for acts of criminality, they may get sent to a Young Offenders Institute. If I could go back in time now and speak to my younger self, I would tell him to turn down the dare, and that's my advice to you, too, dear teenage reader. Nothing good ever came out of someone following through on a dare. Avoid them at all costs during your teenage years, especially if they involve risk, danger, and bending the law.

Chapter Sixteen
ALWAYS LOOK BOTH WAYS

I don't know about you, but I've always wondered what it must feel like to fly through the air like a superhero, catching a falling citizen, a bit like the famous scene in that first Christopher Reeve *Superman* film, where he catches Lois Lane AND a falling helicopter. I always wondered how that felt, knowing that you had saved a person's life? I pondered this until I had the opportunity to do just that...well, kind of.

It was that hot July when I was in Year Ten going onto Year Eleven when I'd go for long walks around London and get into all sorts of trouble with my friends. The cool breeze of those evenings had something magical about them, and I felt that summer was the calm before the storm; we would be sitting our actual GCSE exams in less than a year, with mock exams coming out of our ears beforehand. The headmaster had even said, "This is your last summer of chill," and let me tell you, that scared the living daylights out of me. It was like telling someone they had six weeks to live and then saying, "Have a great summer!"

It was during one of my walks that I found myself walking through the very trendy Camden Town in London. I was by Camden Lock, doing some window shopping more than anything else, occasionally checking my phone to change the song blasting through my wired *Sony* headphones. That probably seems so alien to you kids of the current generation, where you can just double-tap your wireless *AirPods* to change the track. You don't know how good you have it. Trust me on that.

I was walking up to the crossing on Camden Road when I overheard a woman called Julia, who seemed to be in her mid-twenties, talking to a woman named Evelyn, also roughly the same age. They were talking about how Evelyn should just change jobs if she's unhappy. Apparently, Evelyn had a very toxic colleague called Samantha who was spreading gossip, acting like she was better than everyone, and would always stand in the office with a bony hand on her hip, expecting people to greet her. "Just like the witches in *Macbeth*," I thought, chuckling to myself.

Evelyn was in the zone as if she had opened the lid on Pandora's Box and was spilling out all that she had kept bottled up at work. "Honestly, she's a spoilt, manipulative, vindictive little brat, and I can't STAND her. Who the hell does she think she is telling me how to do MY job with those bony fingers and terrible dress sense?"

Evelyn continued to rant non-stop, gesticulating with her hands while looking at the ground as she talked. Her friend Julia listened, walking a few paces behind her, looking ahead as she walked. Julia's responses were reassuring and calming, interjecting with the occasional, "I know, I know, I'm on your side, Evelyn."

It was about a minute into the rant that I heard Julia's voice spike in tone. I was looking at my phone when I heard the panic in Julia's voice, as she cut herself off: "Yes, but I think...Evelyn...EVELYN!"

I looked up to see that while the rest of us pedestrians (Julia included) had stopped at the crossing, Evelyn (unaware of where she was walking during her tirade) had continued to walk and was in the middle of the road. When she heard Julia's primal scream, she looked up and saw the yellow BMW X5 zooming towards her. I saw absolute panic, fear, and terror in her eyes as she desperately looked back to see us all standing on the pavement.

I expected Evelyn to feel everything I saw in her eyes. What I did not expect was her physical reaction: she just STOOD there. That's when it dawned upon me that she was, in a way, paralysed with fear. With her petite frame, long auburn hair, pale skin, and brown leather jacket, she even looked like a little deer caught in the headlights. I mean, at least Bambi ran for it at the sound of gunfire. Evelyn just stood there waiting to be executed by the car speeding towards her.

The pedestrians just watched, too, and I realised there was a very real possibility of us watching the death of Bambi on a busy London road. Maybe it was because it was summer or because I'd watched *Superman* on the TV that weekend, but for some strange reason, the theme tune for that caped wonder came into my mind, and that inner voice inside (the one that usually looks out for you and tells you what to do) told me, "you can save her."

Without a second's hesitation or thought, I ran onto the road, running straight towards Evelyn. I think she noticed me in the corner of her eye because a new emotion seemed to have crept its way in there. Confusion joined her cocktail of emotions, and this sense of confusion grew as I got nearer.

The impact came hard and fast as I collided with her before the car did. Charging at her with my right arm extended, I scooped 'Bambi' up by lifting her off the ground. I continued my run until we were both safely across the road. The whole ordeal lasted about eight seconds.

When I reached the other side of the road, I put 'Bambi' down. By this point, she had retreated into her arms, which she used to shield her eyes. When I pulled away from her, she slowly moved her arms away from her eyes and looked up, blinking several times as she did. By this point, Julia had run across the road and reached us. A shocked and relieved Julia looked down at a shocked and relieved 'Bambi' and said, "Evelyn...this guy just...saved your life..."

Evelyn was too dumbstruck by all that transpired to respond and just stared up at me. That inner voice kicked in again: "Say something heroic and cool, you idiot. This woman will remember this moment for the rest of her life!"

My response was not the best, and don't you dare judge me on it: "All in a day's work...I hope this little incident hasn't put you off walking as it's still one of the best ways to travel in London." Rubbish, I know, but there you go. Poor little 'Bambi' just nodded as if in gratitude and agreement.

I had the heroic moment I'd always dreamt of, but I fell short when I needed to say something memorable. I wish I'd said, "Please look both ways when crossing," as at least this would have stuck with her more and come to mind whenever she came to cross another road. So, impressionable teenage reader, I instead impart that little nugget of advice onto <u>you</u>. Please heed it, as it may just save your life. Always look both ways.

Chapter Seventeen

VETS TREAT PETS, NOT PEOPLE

The title pretty much explains itself, but I think it might be worth elaborating here just a little bit. It was that summer when all things seemed possible, when it seemed perfectly acceptable to climb into zoos, and when it seemed perfectly fine to play superhero on a busy London road.

In August of that incredible summer between Years Ten and Eleven, Imran, Fazlu and I decided we would try and make our own 'stunt' videos – a bit like the hugely popular *Jackass* videos. Now, you may or may not have heard about this slightly psychotic man, dear teenage reader, but the Jackass videos were televised clips wherein American daredevil Johnny Knoxville would put his mind and body through impossible, daring stunts. Some of these were deadly, such as blindfolded skateboarding, while some of them were just plain wrong: in one such clip, Johnny and his team go into a showroom shop like *IKEA* and do a 'number two' in the bathroom on the shop floor – which of course has no water or flush. Disgusting but captivating to watch the reactions of the other shoppers.

Fazlu, Imran and I didn't want to try anything THAT daring, but as I told you earlier, we had bought a camcorder that summer and were pretty excited to use it. I know that for you, this may seem quite lame, but mobile phones were just not the technological marvels they are now. For this reason, Fazlu's camcorder was a pretty big deal, and we all felt like budding videographers.

On a bright, sunny Saturday when it seemed like nothing could go wrong, we took an abandoned *Tesco* shopping trolley that had been left alone on a street weeks ago and headed for Primrose Hill. In our local area, Primrose Hill had one of the steepest hills, and we decided it was perfect, JUST PERFECT, for our first stunt of the week: pushing Fazlu down the hill while he rode the shopping trolley like he was in *Mario Kart*. I mean, what could possibly go wrong?

Now, I won't lie to you. The whole thing seemed like a brilliant idea. That is until we actually REACHED Primrose Hill. We pushed the shopping trolley up to the top of the hill, and when I looked down to the bottom, I said to myself, "Damn, that's not just steep. That is PROPERLY vertical." I started to have second thoughts, while Fazlu was the complete mirror opposite of me. He was PROPERLY raring to go, like one of those bunny rabbits with fresh Duracell batteries in his back or a wind-up toy whose key had been wound back all the way to the end: "Yeah, we're really doing it, man! Is this insane or what?"

It WAS insane, and I couldn't believe I was going through with it. I guess it was due to peer pressure more than anything, as well as the slight sense of curiosity about how it would all go down.

Fazlu eagerly climbed into the shopping trolley, bringing his knees up to his chest and hugging them with both arms. It was go-time. Imran turned on the camcorder and pressed 'record' while I prepared to push Fazlu down the hill.

"Do it!" Fazlu screamed, and I let the trolley go. It slowly and somewhat pathetically rolled down the hill, coming to a slow halt at the bottom. The whole thing was very dull and anticlimactic. I should confess, dear teenage reader, that I had used a fraction of my strength and energy as I was afraid to push Fazlu down the hill with all the strength I had.

Fazlu climbed out of the trolley when it reached the bottom. I could hear the disappointment in his voice: "What the hell was that? You call that a push?"

"Well, no," I said to myself. "No, I don't call that a push, but I also don't want to injure you."

Fazlu was having none of it. "AGAIN!" he yelled, "and THIS TIME, push it AS HARD AS YOU CAN, or I won't speak to you all summer, you little chicken!"

I decided I would just give him what he wanted, as I was slightly annoyed at being called a chicken. This time, I took off my shirt to reveal my white T-shirt underneath, as I wanted my arms to be as lucid as possible to help with the push. I also did the arm stretches we'd been taught in our P.E. lessons and got ready to push him as hard as I could.

"Get in!" I told Fazlu, and he immediately complied. Fazlu knew I meant business this time, and he pulled his knees up to his chest once more, biting onto his T-shirt as if he were preparing himself to avoid biting his tongue.

I'm not happy with my actions, which followed, dear respected teenage reader, and in hindsight, I wouldn't do what I did again.

I took a few large steps back to give myself a little bit of a run-up this time. I ran directly at the trolley as if I were pushing a cursed spirit on a trolley back down to the depths of hell. As soon as my hands reached the handlebar of the trolley, the momentum I had created with my run meant the trolley, and I were speeding down the hill, the speed increasing with every passing second. As soon as I could no longer hold onto the trolley, I let it go, and Fazlu flew down the hill at lightning speed.

As the trolley hellishly sped down the hill, DISASTER struck. Near the bottom, the front wheel HIT a rock that was hidden in the grass, and the trolley flipped forward, PROPELLING Fazlu through the air. Seeing Fazlu in mid-air made me realise that this was no longer a joke. After a few moments of defying gravity, Fazlu came crashing to the ground.

He landed in the grass and let out a YELL that was so high-pitched that we heard it at the top of the hill. Then he stopped moving. We ran down to see if Fazlu was still with us in the land of the living. When we reached him, we saw he was clutching his arm, which was profusely bleeding. Fazlu was yelling in pain, and Imran used his shirt to dab at the blood to see exactly how bad it was. It WAS bad. Fazlu had torn 10cm of his skin, and it was quite deep, not just a simple graze. The minute I saw the blood splattered all over his white shirt, my face went white. I'm sorry, but I was and always have been EXTREMELY squeamish. I have never been able to stand the sight of blood.

With Fazlu in complete panic and with me trying not to throw up, Imran took charge. "Guys, we need to get to the nearest doctor, ASAP." He was right. We got up and started walking, Imran leading the way.

We didn't have to walk far, as Imran led us to a private clinic that he knew about just down the road. "This is good", I thought. Private doctors in London see you on the spot, with no long queues like at an NHS clinic.

This was just as well, as Fazlu had lost a LOT of blood, and he looked like he would pass out at any moment. "Guys, it's right through here, I bring Francis here all the time," Imran said, reassuring us. I'd never met his friend Francis, but if this doctor had treated his friend Francis, then he could treat Fazlu too. I mean, it was only a cut, and all he needed to do was clean the wound and then put a bandage on it.

I remember when we arrived, the logo on the door looked like a weird squiggle. "That's a posh logo for a surgery," I thought to myself, as I dismissed trying to figure out what this squiggle might represent. We went through the sliding doors and right up to reception. We let Imran do all the talking.

"Hi, can I book an emergency appointment to see Dr Kline, please? You can use my mum's credit card. You have it on file."

The receptionist seemed dumbstruck, asking us, "Well, where's Francis?" Her response seemed peculiar. I mean, it was CLEAR that we had Fazlu with us LITERALLY BLEEDING TO DEATH, and she had the audacity to ask where Francis was. Do private doctors only see specific patients? I wasn't sure, but I just did not understand why she would ask what she did when the patient was clearly standing in front of her. We let Imran respond.

"Francis is great. I need Dr Kline to have a look at my friend Fazlu, as he's lost a lot of blood."

Again, the reception responded with a completely nonsensical response, which bordered on racism, "We don't treat his kind here."

I was livid, internally, of course. Like, excuse me? You DON'T TREAT HIS KIND HERE? So, clinics could just be openly racist now? The doctor was all fine with seeing Francis, but poor Fazlu had to go somewhere else? Fazlu was Asian, and I wondered if she was discriminating against him based on his race.

Just as Fazlu's blood was oozing out of his arm, my blood was boiling, and I had a good mind to call out the receptionist on her racism. What stopped me was Imran's response, as he pleaded, "Yeah, I know you won't normally treat him, but can't you just make an exception for Fazlu? He's really hurt, and I had nowhere else to go."

This time I was the one that was dumbstruck. WOW, I thought. Imran just accepted that this was a racist clinic, with institutionalised racism embedded in its systems to the point that it's just a cold, hard reality that visitors must accept. That said, Imran's pleading tone seemed to work, and the receptionist took pity on him. "Okay, boys, just sit down, I'll call Dr Kline out and ask if he will see you."

It would be three minutes before the apparently racist Dr Kline stepped out from the examination room and invited us in. I couldn't believe that we had agreed to see a doctor who discriminated against coloured people, but we had little choice. Fazlu just would not make the journey to a non-racist clinic, as he had lost too much blood.

'Racist Dr Kline' in his racist white lab coat didn't speak after we went in. Instead, he simply cleaned the wound with alcohol wipes and bandaged up Fazlu's arm with the whitest bandages I had ever seen. "God, even his bandages are racist," I thought.

It was only at the end of our makeshift appointment that everything fell into place as Dr Kline finally spoke to us. "Boys, you know that I don't normally treat PEOPLE here..." At that point, I was ready to scream at him about just how horribly racist he sounded (Asian people are people, too!), but his next sentence stopped me.

"This is a veterinary clinic. We treat ANIMALS here, including animals like your dog, Francis. So, the next time you boys pull some mad stunt, call an ambulance, please, before bringing a person into an animal clinic demanding treatment. Enjoy the rest of your day."

I ate the BIGGEST slice of invisible humble pie after he finished, and there was an invisible egg ALL OVER my face. Suddenly, the squiggly logo on the door appeared in my mind's eye and rearranged itself as the silhouette of a cat and a dog standing beside each other.

You can decide for yourself what the lesson is here, dear teenage reader. For me, it was, of course, NEVER to try those "don't try this at home" stunts you see on TV. I mean, that's LITERALLY why they say, "Don't try this at home." I also learnt to avoid making assumptions about people's character. Often, I have found there is an explanation for someone's peculiar behaviour and even their words. It is RARELY (although on some occasions it is) as bad as you think it is. I'd interpreted the receptionist's words as racism because that was the only explanation I could think of with my narrow, world-is-against-me, chip-on-my-shoulder teenage mentality. The truth was much, much simpler.

Chapter Eighteen

DON'T PLAY CUPID

It's always funny when you find out your friend likes a girl, especially when it's in Year Eleven, and your friend starts acting in strange, unexplainable ways. You know what I'm talking about, don't you? *Merriam-Webster* defines a 'Eureka' moment as 'a moment of sudden, triumphant discovery', with this word dating back to *Archimedes*, when he discovered buoyancy. Famously, Archimedes ran stark naked through the streets of the city. When I discovered that my friend Abdul liked a girl in our year named Fatima, I nearly ran through the school shouting 'Eureka' too, trust me.

When you make this discovery as I did, suddenly, everything makes sense. All your friend's strange behaviour can suddenly be explained, such as the fact that he would go all shy and quiet if we passed this girl in the corridor and that his face lit up when the drama teacher put the two of them in a group together. I mean, damn, you'd think he was cast as the lead role in a *Disney* movie judging by the speed at which he moved to huddle with her and her friends!

I didn't make my discovery in Drama, though, oh no. I just put that bit of odd behaviour down to the presumption that he was eager to get into acting later on in life. No, it wasn't in Drama. Rather, it was in Art (of all subjects) that I made my discovery of how absolutely besotted he was with her.

We'd been tasked to either do a self-portrait or a portrait of another student. The winning entry, we were told by our art teacher Mr Horton, would be displayed in the Art corridor. I was quite good at drawing back then, so naturally, I chose to do a self-portrait. This was so that the flawless drawing I did of my flawless face would hang in the school corridor for all to see.

My friend Abdul, however, chose to draw someone else. At first, I couldn't quite make it out; he started with a few strands of hair and a tiny little chin. He then spent twenty minutes on the eyes and then ten minutes on the smile. I swear to you, I thought he was either drawing someone from his imagination or drawing one of the *Spice Girls*. I looked around the room, and I didn't see Scary, Posh, Ginger, Sporty, or Baby Spice anywhere. Actually, tell a lie. I did see quite a few 'SCARY Spices', but the less said about them, the better.

The point is, as I darted my eyes around the room, I saw that there was nobody who matched his drawing. I realised I needed to be in his field of vision. I 'accidentally' dropped my eraser and got up to pick it up from the ground. This gave me the opportunity to stand directly behind him.

I noticed that Abdul was gazing at Fatima, who was sitting diagonal to him, and he looked as if he was in a trance. His eyes were fixated on her. Don't ask me how he was doing it, but without looking away from her and without looking down at his sketch pad, Abdul was drawing her in such fine detail that it would put *Van Gogh* to shame. I don't even think Abdul was blinking, as tiny pools of water had started to collect in the corners of his eyes. Occasionally, he would smile, especially if she made any sudden movements. Don't you dare tell me any of this was cute, dear teenage reader, and if you want to put this book down to go and throw up in the bathroom, please do.

Anyway, let's get back to Abdul and my reaction to him gazing at Fatima – his soulmate. My eyes widened as I realised what was going on, a bit like Joey's eyes did in that episode in *Friends* when he realised Ross got back together with Rachel.

I realised that Abdul was infatuated with Fatima, and it felt like I was privy to a secret that few people knew. Whatever smug face you are imagining me having made, trust me, I had it plastered all over my face. It was like knowing a secret that nobody else knew. It felt good. It wasn't common knowledge, and at that moment, I was the only one in the class who knew about it.

Knowledge is power, they say, and I started contemplating how I would wield this newfound power. Would I use it for good, or would I use it for sheer, absolute evil? Being a teenager, you know more than anyone that I chose to use it for evil, as that's just what teenagers do.

I decided I would embarrass the pants off my friend by going up to Fatima and telling her that Abdul fancied her. Shameful, I know. Absolutely despicable...and yet perhaps I was doing Abdul a favour? Maybe if I told her Abdul liked her, he might actually do something about it, and this might lead them to become the class's golden couple and even get married many years later?

I know what you're thinking, dear teenage reader, and you're right. I had no such long-term goals for them. I just wanted to embarrass my friend, and this is how it went down.

It was Monday, so I decided I would tell Fatima at lunchtime, as that's when the teachers on duty are all distracted 'catching up' with each other about all the boring things they did at the weekend, like looking for two-for-one discounts on clothes that were already cheap. Grandma cardigans, for example.

I saw Fatima standing with her friends in the playground, chatting. "I'll give them all something to chat about," I thought. I walked right up to them and said quite loudly, "Hey Fatima, I don't know if you know, but Abdul LIKES you..." Fatima instantly flushed red with embarrassment. I did not expect what happened next and was therefore not prepared for it. It didn't happen in slow motion like most of my injuries. Nope. It happened in the blink of an eye. In the cold chill of that afternoon in the playground, in front of everyone we knew, Fatima SLAPPED me so hard my cheek went numb. I was mortified! How dare she when all I had done was tell her the truth?

She then burst into tears, and the gravity of what I had done slowly dawned upon me: I'd embarrassed her in front of all her friends and everyone we knew in the middle of the school playground. My words not only humiliated her but also cast aspersions on her character, as there was the insinuation that she liked him too and was maybe secretly talking to him. She probably felt awkward, self-conscious, shy, exposed, and crushed all at the same time, and I was the reason she felt all of those things.

As her friends gave me SERIOUS side-eye, I backed away, mumbling, "I'm sorry, I was just joking." The damage was done, though, and I was too ashamed to speak to Fatima again that year.

In fact, I would not speak to her again for another ten years, when she would pop up on my Facebook. After that fumbled apology so many years back, I apologised properly in the chat and said I was deeply ashamed and embarrassed at what I'd done. She said she accepted my apology but had honestly forgotten about it. Apparently, it had not weighed on her the way it had on me, although she had become a successful businesswoman and launched a dating app called *Love and Relationships* to help young people find love. The app tells a user (and ONLY the user) if another user likes them, allowing them to connect. Many years ago, I'd got it wrong by doing that to her in public. She was getting it right by telling the user (and only the user).

The lesson I learnt from all of that, teenage reader, was that you should always look at a situation holistically and from every angle. I was so obsessed with embarrassing my friend that I had not once considered how it might make Fatima feel all those years ago.

Chapter Nineteen

SWIM FOR YOUR LIFE!

I used to hate going swimming as a young child in primary school, and I'm sure you would too if it was at the unholy hour that my swimming lessons were when I was in Year Five. Although it was a break from the normal school day, my swimming lessons were always at 8:30 a.m. I know, tell me about it! My teacher, Miss Awe, made an annoyingly memorable rhyme she would tell us at 3:30 p.m. the day before, "Half-past-eight, don't be late, we won't wait." God, I wished every morning that they would leave without me. The truth is, they WOULD wait for each and every child to be on the school minibus before we set off for Seymour Swimming Pool in Paddington, where we would willingly immerse ourselves in water that was always at sub-zero degrees to witness the miracle of paddling our legs while trying to avoid dying from hypothermia. "Was it that bad?" I hear you ask. Let me tell you, it was worse, especially as we could barely hear the swimming instructor because it was such a big pool, with twenty-eight kids all splashing or screaming (I always did both).

I preamble my episode with this charming recollection of my primary school days to cement in your mind, dear reader, the cold, hard fact that I never learnt to swim.

Despite this undeniable fact, when I was sixteen years old, I still decided to accompany my brothers when they all went cable skiing on a trip organised by my local youth club – probably because the poster looked cool. It had pictures of kids and adults in these James Bond-style wetsuits. It looked AWESOME! Now, call me foolish or idiotic (I've called myself both since then, trust me), but I couldn't let something small and insignificant, such as the fact that I could not swim, deter me from enjoying such a James Bond-style experience, now could I? Absolutely not. I, therefore, set off that bright Saturday morning at 11 a.m. with my brothers and other members of the local youth to try my hand at cable skiing.

I don't know if you've ever tried it, dear teenage reader, but cable skiing is hard. REALLY hard. We were given this 'wakeboard', which is kind of like a surfboard, where you put your feet in and are basically locked in. You're told to hold onto this bar, which is pulled by electronic cables above rather than by a speedboat. I was sixteen years old with everything to live for, so let me tell you, when that cable became taut and pulled me, I held on for dear life. I wasn't the muscular giant I am today, and with my scrawny little arms, I was always fluttering in the wind whenever I arrived at the corner. Fortunately, we were all given life jackets, so whenever our hands slipped and we fell into the water, we would just swim to shore in order to try again.

It was 3 p.m., and I was on my last run. I held on tight and went zipping across the lake. I then (as always) unceremoniously flew off the end when I hit a corner. Splashing into the lake headfirst, I bobbed up to find my elder brother was there, too. "Well, that was fun," I told him.

"Come, let's swim to shore instead of letting these lifejackets carry us. What do you think? You CAN swim, right?"

I was hesitant, but I didn't want to sound like a wuss in front of him. "Of course I can swim! Come, race you to the shore!"

"Wicked", he replied. "Let's throw off these lifejackets. We don't need these." Stupidly agreeing, I, too, took off my lifejacket and tossed it further into the lake, ready to swim to shore with my brother like a REAL MAN.

I knew that officially, according to every single swimming teacher I had ever had, I could not swim, but there was no better time to learn than the present. So, I started 'swimming' (and I use that term loosely, trust me). The strange thing was, no matter how much I 'swam', the shore was not getting any closer to me. I could see my brother ahead, and he seemed to be getting further and further away. "It must be my eyes," I thought. There must be water in them, skewing my vision.

It was five minutes later that my brother, now halfway to shore, alerted me to the life-threatening nature of my predicament. "What the HELL are you doing? You haven't moved!" It was at that point that I realised I had not moved an INCH towards the shore, and I had just spent the past five minutes splashing around, like some over-excited gorilla in a hot tub, listening to the drumming section of *In The Air Tonight* by Phil Collins.

"Oh God," I thought to myself. "I'm stuck in the middle of a lake. I can't swim. I've depleted my energy, and to make matters worse, I've tossed my lifejacket so far that I can barely even see it."

"I thought you said you could swim?" my brother yelled out, and my silence told him all he needed to know about the level of truth in that lie.

I then saw that he started swimming towards me and I realised he was coming to rescue me. Now, he's only three years older than me, but it meant a lot to see him play that hero role and head back towards me. It's a bit like when you come home with a scrape on your knee from a football match, and your elder brother gives you a little rub on your shoulder and tells you, "It's alright." It's almost like that rub on the shoulder heals your knee a little bit and puts you on the road to recovery. Here, in the middle of the lake, I was filled with that same warm, fuzzy feeling that everything was going to be alright. My brother was coming to my rescue.

When he reached me, he locked arms with me, and he told me to swim with my right arm while he supported me, swimming with his left. We were not that different in size, so this seemed a potentially viable solution to the problem. Anyway, I started loosely swimming with my right arm again, and what do you know? We were going nowhere. In fact, I was going under and then pulling him down with me. It was terrifying. I would hear the noise around the lake. The birds, the other kids in the distance, my brother's splashing, and then this would immediately be replaced with the sound of me gurgling. This would be followed by SILENCE as my head dipped into the water, my feet unable to keep me afloat. My brother would pull me up and tell me to kick my feet. I swear to you, I was kicking like there was no tomorrow, but again, I was more like that gorilla in a hot tub rather than a teenage swimmer.

I was slowly drowning, and to make matters worse, I was probably going to take my brother down with me. That is, unless he let go. When I looked at him, I saw that his eyes were darting left and right as if he were unsure of what to do. I think it was at that point that my brother was faced with quite a difficult decision: let me drown...or drown with me. I was dead weight to him, and he knew it.

Fortunately, my brother made neither of these grave choices. Instead, he opted for a third, which was to yell at the top of his lungs, "Help! Somebody help!" Now, do you remember earlier when I was telling you about that warm fuzzy feeling you're filled with when your elder brother tells you everything is going to be alright? Well, this was the complete polar opposite of that. Hearing my brother yell for help was a bit like him telling me, "We're done for. Nothing is going to work out. I can't help or save you, and we are absolutely, categorically going to die out here." There really is something so defeatist about hearing that, and I thought that if he had given up, then I should too.

"Let me take one last look at the world before I sink to the bottom like the *Titanic*," I thought to myself. I bobbed my head up one last time, my eyes stinging from the water, with water even blocking the hearing in one ear. Despite these restrictions to my senses, I swear to God, I heard the *Baywatch* music in full 7.1 Dolby Surround Sound in my mind when the hulking lifeguard — let's call him 'The Rock', stood up in the distance and looked towards us. 'The Rock' was an absolute beast. Maybe it was the water in my eyes, but when he dived, he seemed to do it in slow motion. Now, it would normally take me five minutes to swim to shore when I had the life jacket on, but 'The Rock' reached us in about twenty-five seconds, even though he swam at half-speed in slow motion.

'The Rock' took charge as soon as he reached us. He told my brother to swim himself to shore and told me to lay on my back and paddle my feet. He put his hand under my chin and swam me to shore with just one arm. Yes, you heard me right. One arm.

The whole thing was undignified, let me tell you. When we reached the shore, we were greeted by all the other members of our group, as well as all my brothers. They were all sniggering at the whole situation, and of course, my little brother started singing in almost a low murmur, the opening words of the *Baywatch* theme: "Some people stand in the darkness…" I shot him a well-rehearsed, 'I-will-literally-orphanage-you' look, and he stopped immediately.

In terms of lessons, this is a pretty tough one to call. There are so many blunders and errors to choose from, so where would I even start? Was it not putting the time in to learn to swim as a child, the terrible decision to go to watersports as a non-swimmer, the ill-fated decision to tell my brother I could swim, or the genius idea of throwing off my life jacket when I knew I could not swim? I don't know, teenage reader. You're going to have to figure this one out for yourself, but HONESTY is what I think about most when I recall this event. If you can't do something, just be honest about it because maybe, just maybe, your life may rest on your ability to tell the truth.

Chapter Twenty
ALWAYS BUCKLE UP

They say that no good deed goes unpunished, and trust me, I felt the full force of that when I was in Year Eleven. Imagine facing off against exhaustion, the police, as well as death itself all in the span of a single night, just because you wanted to do a good deed and help your friend out with his GCSE English coursework. Sounds like a lot, right? Well, that night certainly was one to remember, so strap in, avid teenage reader, as I recount to you the events that took place on that awful night.

You know, we all hated coursework during our time as students. For those of you who may not know, coursework is comprised of small assignments you did at home that counted towards your ACTUAL GCSE grade. Many school subjects have done away with this option now, but back then, coursework was like this inseparable shadow that followed you around, always lurking and always watching you when you were relaxing at home. The problem was, the shadow wasn't yours; it was that of your teacher.

Each and every lesson, your teacher would remind you of THE DEADLINE, as if this deadline referred to the actual day of your death. I mean, damn, it was like our teachers were telling us about the apocalypse, Armageddon and Judgement Day, when it came to their coursework deadlines.

In Year Eleven, our new English teacher, Mr Townsend, was no different when it came to reminding his students that 'the end was near'. Balding, middle-aged, and as boring as a television documentary about recycling paper, he would drone on and on about the coursework deadline. "Your coursework is your bread and butter," he would say, reminding us of the looming deadline. "I don't even like bread and butter," I'd think to myself. It's what old men eat.

Mr Townsend wanted an essay on Shakespeare, a piece of creative writing, and a poetry comparison essay from each student. Unfortunately, my friend Imran had not yet completed ANY of it.

Imran was in a state of panic when he came to me, his DNF (Designated Nerd Friend), for help. Now, I wasn't exactly a FON (Full-On-Nerd) back then, but I was good at English, and that was all Imran needed to know. As he explained, "Listen, man, you know I type slowly, so it takes me ages to write. I just need help writing down my ideas. My mum said she will cook for you." I couldn't turn him down, especially as he was pulling out all the stops and offering up his mum's <u>insane</u> biryani. Plus, he was one of my few friends, and I didn't want him to fail.

I found myself at Imran's house until about 11:30 p.m. It was late. Very late. I was exhausted, but we'd got it done. An essay on *Macbeth*, a short story about a man's climb up a mountain, and a comparison of Wilfred Owen's war poems. We were beat, and Imran offered to drive me home in his mum's car. As he was a year older than me, Imran had JUST passed his driving test. He was so eager to drive me home that it just seemed to be the logical thing to do, so I said, "Yes, cool."

Now, I know by the time you are reading this, teenage reader, your world is probably on *Fast and Furious 11* or *Fast 12*, but that year, the FIRST *Fast and Furious* film had just come out, and all everyone wanted to do desperately was be involved in a street race. It was SUCH an exciting time to be on the road.

Imagine the adrenaline and testosterone levels of two teenage boys in a Mercedes in the early 2000s, and you will get the idea. We didn't break any speed limits, but what happened when we reached that T-junction on Capland Street DID mimic one of those insane scenes you see in a *Fast and Furious* movie.

We pulled up at the junction, stopping at a red light. As Imran edged out to cross the junction, a speeding white van came CRASHING into us, and we started spinning as if we were in an action film. "Oh my God, it's happening!" This was my first and only utterance, as I literally thought our car would spin out, flip five times, and explode. We did spin, but not in the way that I expected. All our wheels stayed on the ground, but the car was rotating like crazy, doing insane doughnuts with smoke from the burning rubber billowing IN through the windows. I heard another CRASH and wondered, "What the hell else did we hit?" We spun two more times before we came to an immediate HALT at the curb, which is actually what stopped us.

My heart was beating a hundred times a minute, and I looked at Imran. He was holding his wrist, which seemed floppy. Almost instinctively, I patted down my own arms and legs, and I'll be damned: I was fine. I looked down and realised we had both buckled up. It was probably the seatbelts that saved our lives. It was at that point that I heard other voices. These voices were confused and angry. When I looked up, I realised where they were coming from and saw what we had hit.

During our insane doughnuts on the road, we had inadvertently HIT a police van that was parked on the side of the road. These two Metropolitan Police officers were, I kid you not, having doughnuts while reading *The Sun* newspaper when two teenagers (us) came crashing into them. We had completely obliterated their headlights and then seemed to park onto the side of the road as if nothing had happened.

I heard one officer shouting to the other, "What the HELL just happened?" They stepped out, inspected their lights, and started walking over to us. They even adjusted their hats like they do in those police shows. Imran and I gulped. I'd never been arrested before, and I didn't fancy life in prison. I mean, I was a passenger, right? There was no way they could arrest me, right? RIGHT?

When Imran rolled down his window, he offered the police officer his driving licence, but surprisingly, the officer did not take it. Instead, he spoke first into his radio before telling us what was going to happen. He spoke plainly with a hit of annoyance in his voice. "Gentlemen, as you, my partner, and I have been involved in a collision, OTHER police inspectors have been dispatched to (he sighed while rolling his eyes) INVESTIGATE, so just hold tight."

Those other officers came within about five minutes. They checked to see if we were wearing our seatbelts, which, of course, we were. "You're lucky, boys, as that carries a £500 fine." They checked Imran to see if he had been drinking. "Only *7-Up* in his mum's house," I joked, and not ONE of the officers even smiled. They did the same checks with the driver of the white van and also, perhaps most bizarrely of all, the police officers we'd crashed into. Imagine being breathalysed by police officers, and you're a police officer yourself in front of teenagers. How embarrassing.

In the end, they concluded that the multiple collision was nobody's fault; it was just that all three cars had been in the wrong place at the wrong time. Imran's Mercedes (which was actually his mum's) was a total write-off. The entire front had caved in, and if the car had dented five more inches, we would have lost our legs. Yikes. Imran got a taxi home in the end, while his car was taken to the scrap heap. The crash happened just ten minutes from my house, so I just started walking home.

It was as I was walking home that I thought about the chain of events that had transpired. Could the crash have been avoided? "Probably not," I thought. It was just a series of unfortunate events with elements of fortune and good luck thrown in. Such is the mish-mash of all of life's events. What saved us that night, though, were the seatbelts. It saved us from forking out £500 EACH, and more importantly, it saved us from being thrown through the windscreen and onto the pavement in order to be pancaked by our own car. That's probably my lesson here for you, dear teenage reader: always buckle up. It may save your life or may even save you from breaking open your piggy bank when stopped by the police whose riot van you completely and utterly destroy one night.

Chapter Twenty One
STAY HOME ON CHRISTMAS EVE

I grew up watching Christmas films like *National Lampoon's Christmas Vacation*, *The Snowman* and (my favourite) *Jingle All The Way*. This last film stars Arnold Schwarzenegger as an absent-minded father who leaves his son's Christmas present, a *Turbo Man* action figure, to the last minute and then spends all of Christmas Eve running around California looking for the figure, to no avail.

It was December, and I was a teenager who was NOT looking forward to sitting GCSE exams that summer. While I don't celebrate Christmas, I was always fascinated by the chaos and hectic nature of Arnold's shopping experience in the film, and I always wondered what it would ACTUALLY be like to hit the streets of a busy metropolitan city on Christmas Eve. Would I get lucky? Would I bag a last-minute deal? There was only one way to find out, and that was to hit the busiest shops that night: *Selfridges*, *Harrods*, and *Hamleys*.

At 4:30 p.m. on that chilly, festive night, I walked onto Edgware Road and headed towards Oxford Circus to see what chaos and craziness I could possibly witness and, most importantly, what last-minute deals I could snag.

I didn't have to go far to find such a deal, which literally presented itself to me in the form of a man in his thirties who emerged from behind *Barclays Bank*.

"Hey kid, you looking for a last-minute present tonight?"

I tried to stay cool, calm, and collected. "What you sellin'?"

"I got the best watches on the market, and they're yours for a small price."

I know. The whole thing sounded dodgy, and as you well know, earlier on in my life, I'd watched my elder brother get duped over a laptop and a camcorder. I was not about to make the same mistake, and I was assured by the fact that this street merchant was not in a car. I told myself that if he tried to make a run for it, I would be able to chase him down. This is because back then, I was pretty fast, if I do say so myself. I could beat

ANY London bus from one bus stop to another, with time to spare. In fact, I'd often do that and ALWAYS got a round of applause from all the passengers.

Anyway, the mysterious merchant brought out these fancy-looking watches from inside his coat.

"They're his-and-her *Swiss* watches, my friend, and they're yours for a penny..." They were silver and really shiny. They had the official *Swiss* watch logo on them, which also appeared on the box.

I looked at the watches, and they looked really good. "One for me and one for my mother," I thought. I asked him how much they were and he gave me what he said was a reasonable price: "£200, so that's £100 each."

It didn't sound reasonable to me. "That's a bit steep, isn't it?"

"Well, how much did you have in mind?"

"How about £40, so that's £20 each?"

After some negotiation, the merchant agreed to my price. The price-drop SHOULD have got me to question the legitimacy of the products, but it didn't. Instead, it just led me to think that I was REALLY good at negotiating. Naivety personified, that's me.

The next moment, 'the handover' was CRUCIAL, I told myself, as I did not plan on getting ripped off in the middle of the streets on Christmas Eve. I'd rehearsed it in my head, and now I needed to put the plan into action.

I already had £40 on me and planned to hand over the money with my left hand, while taking the *Swiss* watches with my right hand. I'm right-handed, so I planned to hold onto the goods with my strong hand.

Due to my forward thinking, the exchange was as smooth as warm butter on a summer's day. I handed over the cash and got my watches, and we parted ways in a nice, amicable manner. Unfortunately, I'd just spent the only money I'd put aside for the Christmas Eve shopping spree. Despite this, I did want to see the chaos of the shops, so I continued on to Oxford Circus.

Now, I don't know what Oxford Street is like nowadays, but THAT day, it was complete and utter MADNESS. It was pandemonium as people ran from shop to shop to buy those last-minute gifts for their loved ones. As crazy as the chaos on the streets was, it was NOTHING in comparison to what I saw indoors at *Hamleys*.

I saw two parents fighting over a *Buzz Lightyear* figure with their children in a similar argument about whose dad looked cooler. There was a mother RUNNING with a *Nintendo 64* in her hands, while another was standing in a shop corner begging her daughter not to hate her because she couldn't find the *Spice Girl* dolls she had promised her. The mother was the one who was crying, by the way, not the girl.

I know, shocked teenage reader. Online shopping for your generation has meant that there is rarely a scarcity of items, but back then, if you couldn't find an item in a shop, then you were going home empty-handed. There was no option to get onto your mobile phone to check online and order it because mobile phones could not connect to the internet, and online shopping did not exist the way it does now.

It really was a joy to watch, and it was everything I had imagined it to be. In my mind, I heard *It's The Most Wonderful Time Of The Year* by Andy Williams, and the only thing missing was Arnold Schwarzenegger running around asking someone for a *Turbo Man* doll or yelling on the phone, "Put that cookie down!" As fun as the night was, though, by 9 p.m. I decided it was time to head home, and that's exactly what I did.

When I stepped through the door of my house, the warmth of all the radiators of the house hit me like an oven. I was really excited to gift Mum her *Swiss* watch. When I walked into the living room, she was sitting with all my brothers watching a film, *Indiana Jones and the Last Crusade*.

Streaming did not exist back then, so you really were at the mercy of what they were televising across channels one to five.

I sat down and told my mother I'd got her a *Swiss* watch. When I gently placed the watch in her hands in all its shiny glory, she was so mesmerised that she would not look away from it, not even to watch Indiana Jones bring his father (played by Sean Connery) back to life.

My brothers, of course, continued to watch the film, ignoring the whole *Swiss* watch situation. That is, except for my elder brother. He casually turned his head and said, almost absent-mindedly, "Here, let me see it."

I walked over and placed it in his hands with the delicacy an expensive *Swiss* watch deserves. He looked it over and turned it over to reveal the back of the watch. Eyeing it up, he threw it back at me, something which took my mother and me by surprise.

"Hey, watch it, that's expensive!"

His response was cold but confident: "Oh yeah? Well it's FAKE is what it is."
"What are you talking about? The *Swiss* logo is LITERALLY on the bezel!"

He responded in that same assured tone, saying, "Yes, but what you needed to do was to check the back of the watch as that should have all the actual logos too, unless it's fake, in which case it's plain, shiny steel." With that, he turned back to the film just in time to watch Indiana Jones ride off with his father into the Jordanian sunset.

I checked the case-back, and there it was: a blank, shiny piece of metal staring back at me, mocking me. In fact, I could see my confused face in the reflection.

"How much did you pay for it?"

"£10," I lied. I know it looks bad, but I couldn't have him knowing how much I ACTUALLY paid as I'd never hear the end of it.

"Well, you may as well have flushed that £10 down the toilet because you just bought a fake watch."

I was devastated and didn't DARE tell anyone about my own one and how Mum and I would now be 'Fake Watch Buddies'. No. Nobody needed to know about that. Instead, I took the watch out of my mum's hands and told her I'd return it. I never did, and I never saw the merchant again.

So, clued-up teenage reader that you now are, avoid going out on Christmas Eve to buy a last-minute gift or to bag yourself a 'bargain'. It's chaotic, psychotic, and you may just find yourself a victim of daylight robbery, where you willingly hand over your hard-earned pocket money in a desperate attempt to buy something that will most likely be overpriced, broken or, worst of all, fake.

Chapter Twenty Two
ONLY HELP THOSE WHO DESERVE IT

One of the first pieces of advice I ever remember an adult telling me is, "Be helpful, kind, and courteous." I carried this all through my childhood, and it got me LOTS of praise. I'd always have family members and even teachers telling me, "You're such a good boy." As a child, receiving praise felt SO special, and it was almost as if someone was telling me that I was better than all the other children. It's a GOOD feeling, and for that reason, I continued to be helpful well into my teenage years. That is, until I was seventeen and realised one of the awful truths of life: you should only help those who deserve it. I realised this truth during an encounter with a classmate, and I wanted to impart this advice to you. I therefore thought I would narrate my account to you, respected teenage reader, in the hope that you learn this cold, hard lesson earlier than I did.

It was that January when we were completing our AS Studies, and we had an upcoming early-entry exam on William Shakespeare's *Othello*.

Now, of all of Shakespeare's plays, *Othello* is one of the most complex, as it involves jealousy, betrayal, and an amoral character that is so innately evil that even by the end of the play, he does not reveal his intentions for doing what he did. It was quite a difficult text to write an exam paper on. The class was struggling to understand the play, and the exam expected a student to respond to critical interpretations of the play. Our teacher, Mr Hayden, only ever gave his own interpretation in lessons, and he acted as if that was the gospel truth. There was no room in lessons for considering differing interpretations of the text, even though that was what the exam demanded.

Fortunately, expecting A-levels to be difficult, I started revising really early. I also had a secret weapon in the form of *York Notes: Advanced* for each of the texts we were studying, which I bought from *Waterstones* as soon as I started my AS in English. This gave me the edge I needed. The York Notes for *Othello* analysed each scene from multiple angles. In the run-up to the exam, I KNEW I would smash it, and unlike everyone else, I was actually looking forward to the exam.

The thing is, I have and always have been cursed with empathy. I say 'cursed' because it really does push you to do things you shouldn't, like helping those who do not deserve it. I did not just want to pass my exam on my own. I wanted EVERYONE in the class to pass the exam alongside me so we could all celebrate the win together.

It was for this reason that I stupidly and naively asked Mr Hayden if I could take the class that Monday morning. Now, it was 9 a.m., and poor Mr Hayden was literally DONE with helping us try to understand *Othello*. He knew HE understood it, but he just could not transfer that understanding to us, no matter how hard he tried. Thus, when I asked him if I could take a portion of the lesson, he JUMPED at the opportunity.

I was actually shaking when I found myself standing in front of the WHOLE class. You know, I'd never been on THAT side of the learning experience before, and I wondered how on EARTH teachers did it on a daily basis. I saw a variety of eyes in the classroom staring back at me: bored eyes, hopeful eyes, pessimistic eyes, scary eyes, critical eyes, and some (although I did not know it at the time) JEALOUS eyes.

I decided the best way to approach it was to talk as if I were just talking to ONE person. Try to save at least ONE life, I thought, from the death grip of the upcoming exam. I looked at the only person that was actually listening attentively because he knew what I had to say was gold dust. This was my friend Wilson, who I could always count on for support.

Not expecting anyone to join him as he listened, I started explaining Shakespeare's play from a feminist perspective, and then you know what? A funny thing happened. The other students in my class ACTUALLY started opening their notebooks and writing down what I was saying. It was a feeling like no other. It wasn't pride or arrogance; it was a feeling that I MATTERED, and that what I had to say MATTERED. In fact, that very moment probably influenced me to grow up and become the outstanding teacher that I am now.

About five minutes in, I noticed that the WHOLE CLASS was taking note of what I was saying. The whole class, that is, except Carlton, who just sat there with an annoyed expression on his face as if he'd just tasted sour milk. I would later find that I was his sour milk, leaving a feeling of distaste and disgust in his mouth.

I spent about twenty minutes discussing the play with the class, giving them the tools to at least PASS the upcoming exam. By the end of my little session, I felt I'd done my duty. I wouldn't be the ONLY person passing now, I hoped, and this actually felt good.

I had no idea that there was anyone with ill intent in my crowd until my friend Imran came to me later that day and told me what he had overheard in the playground. "Don't get mad," he started, "but I heard Carlton mouthing off about you, and I swear I was so annoyed I wanted to punch him."

I didn't get it. "What do you mean, mouthing off about what?"

"Well, he was telling the guys that YOU think you're a big shot because you're a KNOW-IT-ALL, and you think you're better than everyone, and that's why you took today's English lesson."

I was genuinely quite hurt by this. That's the thing about betrayal: its very nature is such that you don't see it coming as it approaches you from behind to give you a gut punch. I felt betrayed and hurt by a person that I was genuinely trying to help, and there he was, talking behind my back and spreading rumours. Don't worry. I didn't start crying or anything, but between you and me, I felt quite upset.

I was torn between confronting Carlton, with his stupid glasses and fuzzy hair, or just leaving him alone and doing nothing about it. In the end, I decided that it would be best just to leave him alone and act as if I didn't hear about his back-chatting and backstabbing acts of betrayal.

I would not hear from Carlton again until two months later when we would get our exam results. I got an A along with my friend Wilson, while the rest of the class struggled with the test and did not get the grades they wanted. The exam was HARD, like I told you, but the good news was that this was an early-entry exam, meaning the class could do it again in June.

I won't tell you about the grades the rest of the class got, but I will tell you that Carlton got a grade E. That's right. Mr First-Name Backstabber, Second-Name Betrayal got what was coming to him. He clearly hadn't heeded my advice and had paid the price, but that wasn't the end of it.

On the afternoon that we got given our results, Carlton came to find me. As I sat in the Sixth Form common room at lunchtime, I saw him slowly walking towards me. Let me tell you, the guy came with his tail between his legs. It almost seemed as if he half knew that I knew he had been gossiping about me but wasn't sure. He also seemed to be ashamed to be coming to me, almost as if he was coming to me as a last resort. His voice was barely a whisper.

"Hey man, I wanted to ask if you could...er...do that Shakespeare session again? Like a crash course, like you erm...did last time?"

The audacity. Literally, the AUDACITY. I mean, oh my God! Mr Backstabber literally thought he could talk behind my back, gossip about me about TRYING to help the class, and then, after failing the exam, come and ask me to help him?

As he stood there in front of me, a PLETHORA of responses came to mind: "Serves you right," "You got what you deserved," "I hope you fail it again and keep failing for all of eternity," and my favourite, "INSTANT KARMA."

However, in the end, I replied with none of these. Instead, putting aside my anger, my rage, and sheer disappointment in him, I simply responded with, "I'm done with that Shakespeare exam, dude, and I got my other exams to revise for, but I wish you the best of luck with it." I'd always heard the proverb being used by others, but it was at that very moment when I truly appreciated its meaning: revenge is a dish best-served cold.

So, dear teenage reader, my advice to you is to be mindful of those you help. You may wish to help everyone, but you will find time and again that you absolutely CANNOT help everyone. You will encounter your own 'Carltons', who may resent the help you offer. What I want to tell you is: don't let them wear you down. Help those you can and help those that are deserving of help.

Chapter Twenty Three
MIND THAT BAG!

Now, I don't know about you, dear teenage reader, but I've always struggled with my school bag, which seemed to have gotten heavier and heavier with each passing academic year. We didn't have lockers back in my days, and this meant you had to carry ALL your school books for ALL your subjects ALL day. To make things worse, if you had P.E. that day, then you were dragging two bags around.

As I said, I struggled in Year Seven to carry my backpack around and always bumped into walls, people, and even doors. I felt like a turtle and not a *Teenage Mutant Ninja Turtle* that was acrobatic, but an actual turtle. I knew that if I fell over, I would not be able to get up without assistance, and I'd be darned if I asked another kid to help me up off the floor like some kind of invalid pensioner. Also, running was basically impossible, and those first few months helped me realise that for each and every turtle in the world, the struggle was real.

I, therefore, changed it up halfway through Year Seven, swapping the backpack for a messenger bag, which I could carry around in one hand, like a pizza delivery bag. The good thing about this kind of bag was that I could see the satchel, and I could always switch hands if it became too heavy in one hand. It was convenient, and it allowed me to run, too. The only downside was that while it did make running easier, I did bump into people with it as I did, and this happened a lot. I was always hitting people's knees, legs, and arms as I ran past them, screaming, "I'm sorry!" as I ran off without turning back to see who it was that I had injured.

This happened all through lower school in Years Seven to Nine and even in my new school in Years Ten to Twelve. This was where things would come to a head, having finally reached boiling point while I was blissfully unaware.

It must have been November when I was in Year Twelve, having returned to school to start Sixth Form when it happened. One of the coolest things about being in Sixth Form in my school was that you were allowed to wear your own clothes. Having spent five years in two different uniforms,

I RELISHED this. I really felt like an adult, as it almost felt like going from a uniformed police officer to being promoted to CID.

We were also allowed out of school at break time and lunchtime, and being out of uniform, let me tell you, we took advantage of this, too. Every day, lunchtime was just another opportunity to go exploring for new coffee shops and lunch spots. It just so happened that on one of these occasions, I would be confronted with my greatest enemy, of whom I was completely, totally, and blissfully unaware.

I was at *Café Nero* near my school with a few of my new Sixth Form friends, and we were ordering coffee like real grown-ups. As we stood in the queue, this guy that I did not recognise came and tapped me on the shoulder. He looked about our age. He was wearing a white T-shirt and a brown jacket with blue jeans. He had messy black hair and long sideburns, which accompanied an angry facial expression. For this reason, let's just call him 'Hugh Jackman'.

'Jackman' asked me if I could help him with something outside. He added that he wanted me to follow him out of the coffee shop, to which I agreed.

I know. Silly move, right? The thing is, this was normal for me back then in the sense that as I was the Sixth Form Student Ambassador, students were always asking me to help them with things, even students that I did not know. I guessed that 'Jackman' was new to the Sixth Form and had something urgent he needed help with.

I followed him out of the coffee shop, telling my friends I'd be right back. The strange thing was that after he exited the coffee shop, he kept on walking until he reached the huge industrial-sized recycling bins behind the coffee shop. I was confused but also intrigued: had he broken his bike or something and needed help putting the wheel back on? This WAS a little beyond my scope as Student Ambassador, but I thought I'd help a fellow student.

After he reached the bins, 'Jackman' started taking off his jacket, and there was no bike in sight. What was this? Did he want me to teach him to dance, or was he going to teach me? The truth of the matter was actually far worse. After he took off his jacket, he started flexing his arms and rotating his shoulders as if he were about to go swimming. This was officially bizarre and beyond any possible guess I could make. At long last, he spoke: "Okay, man, let's go."

I was literally dumbfounded. "Erm, go where?"

"Let's GO. You wanted a fight, so let's DO THIS!"

I held my hands up to indicate I needed an explanation. "Okay, okay, dude, but before we get into this, please, can you explain what's going on?"

He decided he would clarify. "Listen, for two whole years in Years Ten and Eleven, you RAN past me, deliberately hitting me with your bag – on my arms, my legs, sometimes my back, always yelling something as you ran off..." I couldn't believe where this was going. 'Jackman' continued on his angry rant.

"Yeah, and I was gonna deck you last year, but then it was Year Eleven, and you left. I thought, oh well, but then this morning, you had the AUDACITY to come back to Sixth Form, and then you hit me AGAIN, and I thought... this is it. So, you got my attention, so let's get this over with!"

As he spoke, I thought back to all the moments I accidentally hit people with my bag, and I realised a fair few of those times it had been this angry-looking 'Hugh Jackman'. I had to intervene for myself, if that makes sense.

I spoke slowly and methodically so that this hulking wolverine could hear me. "Okay, not to chicken out of this fight with you, dude, but I've got NO beef with you...I've been hitting people for YEARS with this bag by accident. It's honestly nothing personal, and I'm really sorry, dude. I had NO idea. If you still want to fight, though, I'm all for it."

This seemed to calm him down, at least slightly. "For real? You've been doing it by accident?"

"Yes, bro, and I'm sorry. It's been my curse. I've lost a lot of friends over it, and now it looks like I almost got into a dumpster fight over it, too."

'The Wolverine' calmed down and picked up his jacket. "Okay, man, we're cool. Just mind that bag, though, yeah?"

I nodded, and we both walked out from behind those bins. It was a close, somewhat uncanny situation, but I managed to talk 'the Wolverine' down from a bare-knuckle brawl with me behind a coffee shop.

Now, you might be wondering what the lesson is in all of this. Is it to just succumb to the use of a backpack and avoid using a messenger bag at all costs? Well, no. I think it goes deeper than that. I think the lesson has nothing whatsoever to do with messenger bags and backpacks. The lesson here, I believe, is to be mindful of how you treat those around you and mindful of those you might hurt or injure, emotionally or physically, knowingly or unknowingly. For two straight years, I hit and bashed a guy

I had no idea I was hitting and bashing. He, on the other hand, had a growing sense of hatred towards me, each hit with my satchel feeling more personal than the other. This came to a head when he offered to fight me outside a coffee shop, this fight being the culmination of the resentment he had allowed to fester inside him because of my actions. He was absolutely certain that I was hitting him on purpose and wanted to settle this long-standing dispute with his fists. My advice, dear teenage reader? Just be mindful of how you treat others around you, lest you find yourself behind a coffee shop with an angry-looking 'Wolverine' like I did.

Chapter Twenty Four
DON'T FALL IN LOVE

I'm just going to state this as plainly and as clearly as I can, dear teenage reader: don't fall in love until you're about twenty-five to thirty years old. It is the worst kind of self-harm and self-imposed torture you can experience, especially when you're a teenager and your emotions run high. Now, don't get me wrong – those first few weeks feel like a rollercoaster of emotion, and at times, you will literally feel like you're floating in the clouds. Staying with that image of a rollercoaster, though, you and I both know that as much as it goes to dizzying heights, crazy twists, and corkscrew turns, eventually, every rollercoaster comes right back down to ground level. As frightening as that moment is on a rollercoaster, it is a hundred times worse when you experience love's answer to it: heartbreak. What's heartbreak, I hear you ask? It is when that rollercoaster of emotion comes whizzing down past hell itself to depths of depression you never knew existed.

No matter what people tell you, EVERY relationship experiences some kind of heartbreak, a moment where your significant other disappoints you or just breaks up with you with an emoji, not even a text. In those moments, you feel as if the love of your life has plunged their hand into your chest, ripped your heart out while it is still beating, thrown it to the ground, and then trampled all over it. That's what heartbreak is, and I can already feel a lump in my throat starting to gather as I recount my own episode of high-school heartbreak drama to you.

I'd just turned eighteen in January, and it was now April. The typically rubbish British weather had started to show signs of promise, as mornings started to give us rays of sunshine and flowers had started to blossom. We were well into our A2 studies when a new girl arrived at our school. Now, in my school, where the year group and classes had remained unchanged since Year Seven, a new student's arrival was a BIG DEAL, especially when she looked like our new girl did. Her almond-coloured eyes sparkled, and her silky brown hair seemed to have a permanent, invisible fan being blown at it at all times, even indoors. Also, her smile? Yeah, it was to die for, especially as it would bring out a single dimple in her left cheek that made you wish she'd never stop smiling. To me, she was literally *Kim Kardashian* before Kim Kardashian ever even existed. For the purposes of this story, though, we will give her the name I gave her back then: 'Dream Girl'.

All of us boys just gaped at her when she walked into our English class wearing her perfect scarlet jumper and casual denim jeans, and all the 'mean girls' just folded their arms as their eyes went into 'attack' mode. 'Dream Girl' was a new threat, and they had to make sure she didn't upset the hierarchy they had spent years establishing.

I knew right there and then that she was the one for me. In my mind, she had moved to that school FOR ME, and it was written in the stars. Destiny, just like *Romeo and Juliet*. I had to find an opportunity to talk to her, but in that first lesson of the day, no opportunities presented themselves. So instead, I just did what every teenager does, and don't pretend you haven't done it yourself: I just STARED. I remember turning to my friend David and saying something along the lines of, "Man, she's FLY."

David's response was on point: "You can say that again, dude."

Sixth Form students spent free lessons in the Common Room, and I decided I would use that time to introduce my wonderful self to her. All I needed to do was tell her my name and say something witty while I pushed my fingers back through MY silky hair (that was my secret move back then), and she would instantly fall for my dashing good looks and charm. Well, that's what I told myself.

I was free for the fourth lesson of the day, so I headed out to *Army and Navy*, a department store just down the road. On the first floor of the shop, they had a perfume section for men and women, complete with those little 'tester' bottles for customers to try. Now, don't judge me for what I did because I reeked of my Lynx Africa body spray. I hadn't put on any perfume at home as I did NOT expect the girl of my dreams to walk into my life that day. Lynx is fine for school but not for charming your way into someone's life. If she were to fall in love with me, I couldn't smell like every other boy in the school. I needed an EDGE and needed to smell like a BOSS. *Hugo Boss*, to be precise.

I, therefore, sprayed myself silly with the new *Boss* fragrance. I then used one of the hairbrushes in the women's make-up area on the way out (DON'T JUDGE!) to fix my hair into place and walked back to school, smelling and looking like a millionaire. I was irresistible, and she was going to be putty in my hands.

When I got to the Common Room, my heart was racing. I stepped in and saw 'Dream Girl' sitting in a corner, looking at her timetable with a slightly confused look on her face. I walked over and leaned on the wall in a position that was neither natural nor relaxed.

"Hey, how you doing? Is that timetable bothering you? Shall I make it go away?" I mentally kicked myself. I was NOT a smooth talker, clearly, but it worked. She looked up and smiled.

Her voice was like melted butter. "You know what, it's...confusing, it doesn't say what rooms the lessons are in," she replied, not looking up from her timetable. She needed a knight in shining armour, and here I was, I told myself.

"Can I borrow it for five minutes? I made my own electronic timetable on my laptop with the room allocations, and I can just edit your details on it."

"Sure! Oh my God, you're so smart! That would be wicked."

I swear to you, my heart skipped ten beats, and I almost passed out. She had COMPLIMENTED me in our first interaction. She'd said I was SMART, an intellectual, right up there with the likes of Edison and Einstein. She valued my MIND, and that's the kind of relationship that lasts forever. FOREVER.

I opened up my laptop and had her new timetable emailed to her within four and a half minutes. She beamed at me when I told her the new timetable was in her inbox. As she was sitting across from me in the Common Room, she blew me a kiss and mouthed two words that I replayed in my head the whole day: "My hero." I immediately imagined myself in a flowing red cape like *Superman*, rescuing her as she fell thirty floors of confusion in the new school.

That day, as I headed home from school listening to the radio on my *Sony Walkman*, there was an extra spring in my step. Not only that, but all the songs I heard that day HIT DIFFERENT. It was as if each and every love song that played on 95.8 Capital FM was written with me and 'Dream Girl' in mind. Backstreet Boys' *As Long As You Love Me*, Britney Spears' *Baby One More Time* and even Beyoncé's *Crazy In Love* were all about the love I had for my beloved 'Dream Girl' and the love she clearly had for me too, her HERO.

In fact, it was these love songs that helped me to plan out my life with 'Dream Girl' as I sat in bed that night. In my mind, we would both finish college, go to the same university, get married, and both be employed in our dream jobs, making waves in the wide world of work.

By the end of the week, after some carefully crafted conversations in the Common Room, I was sure she liked me back. I mean, on numerous occasions when I was talking to her, she'd said, "You're SO smart...get out of here, dude!" She wouldn't say that unless she liked me, right? RIGHT?

I used that weekend to get a fresh haircut and bought a new navy blue shirt. I planned to tell her, on Monday morning, that I liked her, like REALLY liked her. I also BOUGHT that *Hugo Boss* aftershave I'd used in our first encounter and spent ages rehearsing how the conversation would go. I won't bore you with the details, as it is way too embarrassing, and there is more of this book to read. I can't have the cringe-metre skyrocket right now...not yet, anyway. Plus, you better prepare yourself for the next bit of news because what happened next was...well, you probably already guessed it: heartbreaking.

Did she let me down gently? Did she tell me, "You're smart and funny, but I don't like you back?" Sadly, no. It was worse than that. Much, much worse.

I am pretty sure I skipped to school that day, jumping between imaginary clouds, which paved my way to my great love. My heartbeats quickened as I neared the school gates, and the Sixth Form Common Room loomed ahead.

I bought some flowers from the local supermarket. With the flowers in hand, as I went through the blue door and stepped into the Common Room, my heart sank at what I saw, and my smile faded. My friend David and 'Dream Girl' were holding hands and laughing. I could barely breathe, and it felt like my asthma, which I'd had as a kid, was coming back. When Imran noticed me, he walked right up to me. "Hey, check out the golden couple, David didn't waste any time." Nope. He didn't. I did. I'm the one that wasted time and missed my opportunity. I'm not being dramatic, but thank GOD I was young, or I would probably have had a major heart attack right there and then and died on the spot. A single tear streamed down my face, mourning the life with her that would never come to pass.

I don't think I ate much the rest of that day. It felt like David and 'Dream Girl' had both trampled all over my heart. I mean, it wasn't David's fault. I never even told him I liked the girl as I was too busy getting my act right to impress her. David? Well, in the end, he just wowed her by being his wonderful self. That didn't make what happened any less painful, though.

The sad thing was, I didn't get to tell the girl that I liked that I liked her. Now, she was with David, and I would just have to accept that, which I did. The irony is, after a month, 'Dream Girl' moved schools again. She went to a local all-girls school and was out of our lives before we knew it.

During those few weeks that followed, each and every 'break-up' song that was played on the radio was about ME, and the worst thing was when radio stations decided to play 'Golden Oldies', such as Tony Braxton's *Unbreak My Heart*. I swear to you, it almost seemed personal, as if the DJ knew what had happened to me and was just playing it as his own form of torture.

The whole ordeal taught me just how painful heartbreak can be. At the same time, it taught me that liking someone really is a feeling like no other. I mean, there is a REASON there are so many songs that are written about it. When I first met Dream Girl, I was on Cloud 9, and nothing on earth could beat that feeling. I would want to go to school just to see her. Being the grown-up, wise man I am today, I know what I felt or experienced back then wasn't love in the sense of enduring love, but it was literally a case of boy meets girl, boy gets his heart broken. I didn't really love her as I didn't know her, but I really did like her.

So, my advice to you, teenage reader, is to try and avoid falling in love or even liking someone in your teenage years at ALL costs unless you are ready and prepared to have that heart ripped out and shredded to pieces as a result of the accompanying and inevitable heartbreak which follows it.

Chapter Twenty Five

DON'T GO ON A GAME SHOW

My advice? Don't go on a television show. Don't even dare. I know that being a teenager fills you with a daring sense of confidence you can only DREAM of when you're older (it fades, trust me), but deciding to go on a television game show is the ultimate display of hubris that you could LITERALLY do without. So, don't do it, and let's just leave it there for this episode...

What's that, dear reader? You ACTUALLY want to find out why I'm saying this? You want to discover what I did on television that was so embarrassing? Fine, but let me warn you in advance about the level of cringe and discomfort involved in this story.

It was the summer after I'd completed my AS Studies, and I'd just achieved 3 A's for my AS levels. I was halfway to securing my place at Queen Mary University of London. I just needed to get 3 A's again for A2, which seemed like a walk in the park.

It was the morning after grades day, and I won't lie; I felt pretty intelligent and pleased with myself. I was having my morning cornflakes when a quiz show, *Brainteaser*, appeared on television. Now, I know that this show is no longer on television, but back then, before streaming and before digital TV, back when we ONLY had five channels, *Brainteaser* was quite big. It was a show on which, as the adverts stated, "Contestants answered general-knowledge questions for a chance to win big money." That morning, the questions seemed easy, and I even answered a few of them before the contestant.

At the precise moment of the first commercial break, having achieved three A's in two consecutive years AND having been crowned the smartest boy in the school, I decided I would try to win myself some big money on the game show. I mean, I could definitely do with the cash at university, so I rang up the number advertised after the break and signed up to be a potential contestant. I then had to leave my mobile number on the automated machine and await a call from the studios.

I would get a phone call three days later while I was out buying some bubble gum. What can I say? I felt like some bubble gum that afternoon. Sophie, one of the assistants for *Brainteaser,* told me the good news, "We are excited to let you know that you might be next week's contestant!"

I was overjoyed. "That's great news. Okay, just email me the location of the studio, and I'll be there!"

Sophie continued. "Yes, we just need to check how good your general knowledge is, so I will ask you some quick-fire questions now and see if you can answer them. Ready?"

I gulped. I felt a growing sense of panic as I realised that aside from academic knowledge, my general knowledge was absolutely rubbish.

I needed a plan and quick. Now, you need to remember that mobile phones back then did not have the internet. We just weren't there yet as a society. I knew this, but so did Sophie. The needle on the panic-o-metre was steadily moving and was about to reach the highest point of "IT'S OVER." What could I do? I was literally in the streets about ten minutes from my home computer, and I couldn't start asking random pedestrians to help me.

As I darted my eyes around Church Street, I noticed the sign for the public library. Church Street Library, to be precise. It was thirty seconds from where I was, and it was open. Aside from books, Church Street Library also had computers connected to the internet, which users could book, and I just so happened to have my library card number memorised. What? Those three A's didn't achieve themselves, you know. I was a geek, and at that moment, I was glad that I was.

I needed to stall Sophie as I fast-walked to the library, so I just started waffling: "Of course, Sophie! I'd LOVE to answer some general-knowledge questions. You know, I'm something of a general knowledge master, and this has been the case since I was a small child, when my grandfather would hold quiz nights whenever we visited him..."

Sophie was a bit taken aback by this autobiographical outburst. "Okay...are you ready?"

I was. During that short rant, I'd got into the library, logged in by silently typing my details with one finger, and had the popular search engine *Ask Jeeves* open. I had also connected my mobile phone to my wired headphones so I could type with both hands, carefully and silently of course – criminal mastermind, clearly.

"Go for it, Sophie."

"Okay, first of all, when was George Washington President of America?"

Wow. Thank God I was on the internet, as that was a real whopper of a question. I talked over my stealthy typing, so Sophie thought I was thinking out loud rather than asking the internet, "Oh, good old Georgie! There's a bridge named after him in America, you know! And of course, if I had to guess, I'd say he was President between April 30th, 1789 and March 4th, 1797."

Sophie was stunned. "Wow, that's absolutely right! I was expecting just the years, but you gave me the exact dates I can see on my computer screen!"

"Well, what can I say? I got an A in GCSE History, you know."

"Well, that's great. I've only got one more question for you, and if you get it right as quick as you did this one, we will see you on the show! So, if you're ready, what is the only continent with land in all four hemispheres?"

Great. Geography was my LEAST favourite subject. In a school test in Year Seven, I'd messed up the test SO badly by getting all the names of the continents wrong that they'd called in my parents. Well, Sophie didn't need to know THAT, and I kept her talking as I searched for the answer: "Oh my God, Sophie…Geography! That's my FAVOURITE subject! I am SUCH an environmentalist! By the way, we really should be doing MORE about greenhouse gases. It's something I really believe in. Oh, and before I forget, the answer to your question is Africa, I mean, duh!"

"Congratulations, you're THROUGH! I am going to email you all the details in about ten minutes! See you next week. Please remember to follow all the instructions in our email. See you then, general knowledge superstar!"

Wow, I was through, and I was going to be on television! This would give me HUGE bragging rights at school and at family gatherings. I was literally elated. Of course, I went home and told my family. My mother told ALL the members of my extended family. Aunts, uncles, cousins, you name it. EVERYONE would be tuning into the live episode.

I woke up at 6 a.m. on the day I was going to appear on television. The email informed me to bring glasses if I wore them. 'Yeah, right," I thought to myself. As if I'd willingly appear on television looking like a geek. It also had some instructions about clothing that I chose to ignore. Finally, the showrunner told me to arrive at the studios an hour before the show aired live so they could brief me and go through a full rehearsal.

The studio was an hour's drive, so I took a taxi. I was wearing my favourite jumper and pants, which I'd set aside the night before, so I didn't want to ruin them by using public transport, which sometimes had stains on the seats.

When I arrived at the address sent in the email, I found myself in front of a solid grey door, Studio 63. I buzzed it, and they let me in. When I saw the studio, I was taken aback by it all. As a teenager, I'd never seen the inside of a television studio. I realised there were SO many people involved in a television show, and it wasn't just a host in front of a single camera. It was quite overwhelming, but I was quickly brought down to reality when one of the runners came over and took me to meet the assistants, which included Sophie. I was also introduced to the other contestant, Janice, who was a thirty-five-year-old retail worker at *Sainsbury's*. Sophie briefed us both on how the show would run. I looked at Janice and decided I was smarter than her, as I had just been dubbed the smartest boy in the school. "This is going to be a cakewalk," I thought to myself.

It wasn't. Of course it wasn't. They say pride comes before a fall, and if that's true, then I literally threw myself down into the Grand Canyon of shame and embarrassment due to my pride. The first thing I was told by the assistants was that I had to change my clothes. "We said in the email that you could wear anything but black and white, and you chose to wear black and white."

Darn. I'd skipped over that minor detail. When I told them I didn't bring any spare clothes, they supplied me with this HIDEOUS, creased green shirt they had in the back of the studio. I had to take off my favourite jumper to wear this horrid shirt, and I messed up my hair when I did. My confidence dropped like a lead balloon. I swear to you, the shirt looked like someone had found it in the gutter.

Secondly (and this was the worst part of it), for the scramble challenge, the BIG LETTERS, which appear on the television screen below the contestant, do, of course, appear through television magic. In reality, the contestants must look at a tiny, tiny monitor to see the letters. While I wear glasses now, back then, I didn't, even though I actually needed them. I didn't want to look like a geek on television, and this was going to cost me.

No matter how hard I squinted, I definitely couldn't see the teeny tiny screen in the studio, and this was a real problem. The showrunners came onto the studio floor and asked what the problem was. When Sophie explained, the director of the show (I forget his name) asked everyone who wore glasses to let me try them on.

I tried on each and every pair, drowning in embarrassment as I did. With ten minutes to spare, I finally found a pair I could see with. They were owned by the producer, who was not too pleased that he had to loan out his glasses to a constant, but he reluctantly obliged.

Thus, when Janice and I went head-to-head live on *Channel 5* with my ENTIRE family watching, my hair was a mess; I was wearing a horrid green shirt and geeky glasses that were not even mine. I don't know if it was the embarrassment of being on live television, the crippling fear that I'd used the internet to get onto the show, the glasses, the hair, or the green hue of the shirt, but I honestly felt like throwing up. Don't worry, I didn't. Instead, I stood there as the cameraman counted down the host of the show, Alex Lovell.

In her bright blue suit, Alex introduced Janice and I. The first thing I found was that when Alex asked me what I was going to study at university, my voice, which is usually quite loud and confident, became a whisper. I was terrified and literally DYING of embarrassment. I felt like a mouse trapped in a cage, a mouse that the whole world was watching. I mean, Alex explained to us in the briefing that live television is scary, and she had the utmost respect for anyone who puts themselves forward to appear on it, and she was right. As Alex asked the first question, though, things got worse. A lot worse.

Now, you're probably wondering how on earth they COULD get worse. Well, let me tell you. Remember my little hack of using Church Street Library to answer those general-knowledge questions from Sophie? Well, it turns out that in real life, I had NO general knowledge. None whatsoever. I mean literally zero. I must have fluked those questions I'd answered that morning during the televised episode after grades day because when it came down to answering them on live TV, my mind drew a complete blank. Janice, on the other hand, knew EVERYTHING and was absolutely thrashing me on points. When she was on thirty points, my points amounted to 0.

To this day, I thank GOD that while Janice unscrambled the only word she got stuck on, she could not pronounce the word "philanthropist," which she had unscrambled from PIST PHIL THRO AN. She buzzed in but struggled to pronounce the word.

"Philan...oh, I can't say it. Philant...oh, it's too hard."

Alex tried to encourage her, saying, "You know it, Janice, I JUST need you to say the word!"

Janice continued to struggle, saying, "Philanthropi...oh, I just can't say it. My eyes widened. PHILANTHROPIST!

I saw my opportunity, and I swear to you that I was slamming the HELL out of that buzzer. Did you know it only buzzes ONCE, no matter how many times you press it? I was raining down my hand on it, hitting it over and over.

Alex reluctantly nodded at me. "Philanthropist!" I exclaimed.

Alex had to hold her earpiece to check if the answer would be allowed.

"Erm, okay, yes, we ARE going to let you have that one. Well done – that's five points."

I know it was a pity allowance from the showrunners, who probably felt sorry for me, but I didn't care. At least I'd scored five points and was not going home with zero points.

Those were the only five points I scored for the remainder of the show. As Janice continued to answer questions correctly, I just stood there. I mean, the situation was so dire that when we were asked who played James

Bond in a crossword segment of the show where only the letters E and A could be seen, instead of saying the correct answer, "SEAN Connery," I answered 'Edgar'. Edgar. When did you hear about an actor called 'Edgar' playing *James Bond*?

I went home with a commiseration coffee mug they give all contestants, while Janice went on to win £500, which she said she would use for a holiday to Marbella. Good for you, Janice, good for you.

As I sat on the bus on that long, one-hour journey home, I hoped the bus would take as long as it could because I was not ready to face the endless teasing from my family and friends that would ensue as soon as I reached home.

I also thought about where I had gone wrong. Was it the poor choice of clothing, ignoring the instructions in the email? Was it the fact that I refused to wear glasses even though I needed them, causing a commotion in the studio? Or was it just my lack of general knowledge that caused me to lose so monumentally?

I realised it was none of the above. Well, it was a bit of the above, but none of them were the root of the problem. All the above problems stemmed from the fact that I'd cheated in the beginning and lied. I'd pretended to have an excellent grasp of general knowledge when Sophie had called me. I'd used the internet in the library to cheat my way onto a televised game show. It was only right that I suffered the multiple ways that I did, coming on live television with a disgusting green shirt, messed up hair, and geeky glasses, getting beaten by Janice, who got all her answers right, just as I got every answer wrong.

I told you, dear teenage reader, don't go on television. Don't even think about it. No matter how easy it looks or how smart you may think you are, just don't do it, and definitely do not lie your way onto a show, saying you can do something you cannot. If you are not too careful, you might just end up going live with a pair of glasses and wearing a vomit-coloured shirt like I did.

Growing up, it's important to know your strengths and your limits. We are all human and able to do wondrous things, but we all have limits, too. It's important to know these so that you can lean toward your strengths.

BID A FOND FARWELL TO CHILDHOOD

I started this journey into my teenage years by mentioning that with the death of my father, a small part of me died. It is, therefore, only fitting that I end this glimpse into my adolescent years by recounting to you how something equally real and equally tragic happened to me at age nineteen, just before I went to university, when I almost lost my life due to my own recklessness. This event cemented the idea that I was leaving my boyhood years of naivety behind me and entering into the cold, harsh world of adulthood, where I needed to be constantly vigilant of all the threats around me. I am going to tell you about the time when I almost died, just because I left my homework to the last minute.

It was February, and I was in the second year of my A-levels, just before I headed out to university. Even though coursework deadlines were looming, I'd delayed reading Wordsworth's famous work *The Prelude*, as it was among a pile of other books on that 'Romantic' shelf in my room, stuffed between the works of Coleridge, Mary Shelley and Anna

Barbauld. Needless to say, I planned to get to it among the 1000 other books I needed to read that term. I mean, it's called an English A-level, but goodness me, they expect you to read a lot.

It was not until 11:45 p.m. the night before I was meant to have read it that I picked up Wordsworth's book and realised it was no short read. It had over 736 pages, and my class was at 9 a.m. the next morning. None of the online summaries did it justice, not for the intense discussion Miss Jardin expected of us. She was a real hard nut, and I always felt she was judging me when she looked down at me through those glasses that sat perched on her nose. I couldn't have her judge me for leaving this book to the last minute. I therefore decided I would spend all night reading it if I had to.

I would complete all 736 pages so that when I went into class the next morning, I was fully prepared to quote it verbatim if I had to. I remember finishing that last page of the book at 4 a.m. and then falling asleep on that desk that I shared with my brother.

My alarm clock woke me up at 8 a.m., and let me tell you, I'm pretty sure I threw that alarm clock out the window when it did because I couldn't find it the next day. When I opened my eyes, I felt like I had just been hit on the head with a sledgehammer, the ones that builders used to demolish the insides of houses before detonating the whole thing with dynamite. I was in a trance as I got dressed, and I just seemed to be doing everything at half-speed. This meant I didn't leave my house until 8:30 a.m., and I was running late. Very late.

I got to Victoria Station at 8:55 a.m., and I had five minutes to get to school, which was a ten-minute walk away. I told myself that I had no choice but to run, no SPRINT it there, and that's what I did. There was a zebra crossing halfway down the road, but I decided it would be faster to cut through the four lanes of traffic and get to the other side of the road rather than waiting at some traffic light like a loser. I'm not justifying it to you; I'm just explaining my thought process at the time.

The next bit happened in slow motion, or at least it did in my mind's eye, as every near-death experience does for me. The cars were going at 25 miles per hour, as that was the speed limit on that road. I remember running through the first lane of traffic and jumping between two cars. I jumped through the second lane and was onto the third lane with just one more to go when a red BMW came speeding into me and hit me dead-on.

I heard a crack, and I'm guessing that was the windshield, but what I remember most vividly about that moment was just how blue the sky was that morning. "Beautiful," I thought. People in London rarely take the time to look up at the sky and admire the beautiful skies of this great city, jewelled with white, fluffy clouds. I then realised the reason I found myself looking up at the sky: I'd been hit by a car, my body was completely horizontal, and I was about to come crashing down to both reality and the cold, hard road. I hit it hard with my shoulders first hitting the road, followed by the back of my skull.

I got up, seemingly unhurt or in any kind of pain. Again, there was that dreaded feeling: am I dead? Surely, the Angel of Death was lurking somewhere, ready to take my soul, which by now had to have been completely severed from my mortal body? I turned around and thankfully saw no dead replica. I almost shouted out, "I'm still alive!" I then looked around and realised my collision had brought traffic to a halt on that busy road. I saw the flashing red and blue lights before I heard them, as my ears were still ringing from my head's impact on the road. I saw that the police had cordoned off the road, and there was also an ambulance on site. The police seemed to be questioning the driver, and I felt hands around my shoulders. I looked up and saw that it was the ambulance staff requesting that I come with them so they could get me checked up at the local hospital.

I have always been quite studious since I was a young boy, but I believe my refusal to go straight to the hospital that morning stemmed more from my concussion than from my love of learning. "I would like you to drive me first to school so I can put my dictaphone in the lesson, and then you can take me to the hospital," I told the ambulance staff in quite a delirious and somewhat high-pitched tone.

"We are the London ambulance service, sir, NOT a taxi service."

I scoffed. "Fine, then drive off, and I'll go to the hospital after my class, but tell me, do you want to risk a teenager passing out on the way to the hospital just because you refused to wait for him?" The driver's stunned silence was enough of an answer.

I ran into class twenty minutes late and out of breath. I was dishevelled, and my shirt was covered in dirt from the pavement. The teacher looked down at me, right past those glasses that sat on the very edge of her nose. "Judge me," I thought. I was just there to put my dictaphone down. Plus, she had a right to give me the look she did as I had just barged in twenty minutes late into her lesson.

"You are twenty minutes late, young man. Find your seat."

"Well, Miss, funny story, but I can't stay..."

She raised her eyebrows even higher. "Excuse me?"

"I am trying to explain. Now, you see what happened was..."

She cut me off. "I honestly don't care for your excuse. Now, SIT DOWN!"

She turned her attention back to the other students. As Miss Jardin continued to speak to the class, I turned to Julie, the teaching assistant. I quickly drew a car with four horizontal arrows leading to a stickman, which I labelled 'me'. Julie mouthed, "Oh my God..."

I wrote the words 'AMBULANCE OUTSIDE' in big, bold letters and pointed my head towards the teacher. Julie nodded, showing that she understood, and pointed her head towards the door. With a single nod, she gave me the green light to leave while simultaneously telling me she would smooth things over with the teacher after I made my haphazard exit.

I rushed back to the ambulance and was taken straight to the Accident and Emergency Ward. I was rushed in as a head trauma patient and told that I was being put in for an immediate CT scan of my brain to see if there was any trauma to the brain. "Oh God," I thought. I still had my A-level exams and then university after that. I HAD hit the pavement pretty hard with the back of my head. What if I'd done irreparable damage to my brain?

I apologise for this next reference, but at that age, I made sense of the world through the films I watched. A scene from the not-so-famous *Rocky V* immediately flooded my mind, when Rocky's doctor told him, "You have severe brain damage due to the continuous blows to the head, and the effects are irreversible." What if there was irreversible brain damage and I could not continue my studies? Suddenly, the comedy of the whole situation, of surviving a crash and using an ambulance as a taxi, all faded, and the humour in my mind was replaced with a single, paralysing emotion: fear. Would my life change? Would the damage get worse?

Following the scan, I anxiously waited for the results. I had never had a CT scan before and never had to wait to be told whether or not I had brain damage. I shed a few tears as I waited in the waiting room, just from the shock and horror of it all. I was clenching my fists, as I always do when I am nervous, afraid, or worried, and I could feel my heart literally pounding in my chest.

The noise of the hospital sort of drowned itself out, and you know what, dear teenage reader? I thought about my life, all eighteen years of it. They sort of went by in my mind's eye as I sat in that hospital bed, almost like a slideshow of pictures. I thought of my brothers who weren't there beside me, my school friends, and all the events you've read about in this book.

I thought of how life passes by so quickly and how, in a single moment, it can end, just like that, or how your life can irreversibly change in an instant. Did I have irreversible brain damage? Was there internal bleeding? Would I need surgery? Nothing was certain, and my mind was full of questions, fears, and, as strange as it may sound, memories. I guess that's what they mean by "your life flashes before your eyes" because, in a way, I can tell you that it does both during and in the aftermath of a life-threatening incident. You think of the good, how all the bad in your life wasn't that bad at all, and all the times you got upset with someone over something silly.

You think of all the avoidable arguments you had with your parents and how you would give ANYTHING to just have them there with you now as you lay in hospital, waiting to be told news about your health.

As I sat waiting for the results of my scan, I quietly made some decisions on that hospital bed that day. These are decisions I have never shared with anyone before, but I wanted to share them with you, dear teenage reader, as you have been with me throughout this glance back into my teenage years. I promised myself that if I was given the all-clear, I would go on to finish my English degree and go on to become an English teacher. However, I would not just become ANY English teacher, oh no. I would be the best English teacher ever to walk the face of the planet. If I got to see through adulthood, I would be the teacher my students would never forget because of the learning experiences I would give them in my classrooms. I would travel the world with my teaching, and I would shape myself to become the best human being that I could be. I would grow to become someone people would not forget because he was the kindest, most caring, and considerate person they knew.

I then felt a hand on my shoulder. It was the neurologist. I wish I remembered his name. I remember the two words he uttered, which still give me goosebumps when I recall him saying them: "All clear."

I sat frozen on the bed. I felt like I had been given a renewed lease on life, and I decided that I needed to earn it. I needed to do away with childish foolishness and look at my years ahead with a sense of responsibility and maturity. Considering the antics you have read about in this book, that may sound silly to you, I know, dear teenage reader. But it felt like...I don't know. It was as if being hit by that car was a wake-up call, with the universe urging me to be better, to do better and to leave aside childhood as I embraced adulthood.

Heading home, I received an email from my teacher, Miss Jardin, wherein she expressed her heartfelt apology for being so short with the victim of a car crash, as well as several SMS messages from my classmates, which all read something along the lines of, "Dude, are you dead?"

"What an inappropriate question," I thought. How would I reply if I was? It had been a near-miss, but only just. Childish naivety and foolishness, wherein I had left a 736-page book to the last minute, had almost cost me my life. I had narrowly avoided doing irreversible damage to my body and even my brain, all because of my naïve decision to run across a road to get to school rather than doing the sensible thing of just waiting at the pedestrian crossing.

As the taxi approached my house, I shed just a few more tears, only these were tears of joy. I had been given a second chance at life, and I decided that I would keep those promises I had made myself. I was going to grab life by the reins and give it my all.

It's on this note that I leave you, dear teenage reader, as my life as an undergraduate and then as an English teacher comprises episodes for another book. Before I go, I wanted to thank you for sharing this journey back into my boyhood years, wonderful teenage reader that you are. I hope you can heed at least some of the lessons we've drawn from these episodes in my teenage life, and I hope you will join me in the next book about how to navigate university, the world of work, and life as an adult.

ABOUT THE AUTHOR

Aslom Ullah is a teacher of English who was born and brought up in London. Ten years ago, he came to live and work in Qatar, and it was here that he first started writing. He wrote a song celebrating the 2022 FIFA World Cup, which became an unofficial hit here, garnering over 10 million hits. The lyrics resonated with fans during the entire tournament, and won him a Silver Play Button from Youtube. He has recently started doing educational podcasts, interviewing prominent members of the educational community around the world.

Sound a bit too picture-perfect? Well, Aslom's life wasn't always this rosy. Aslom grew up in London in the late 1990s. This was before social media ever existed. The internet could only be accessed in public libraries and home PCs, and when a mobile phone the size of a brick could not even take a picture. Needless to say, life was hard, and in navigating his teenage life, Aslom fell into many pitfalls. Some were purely accidental and could happen to anyone (such as burning down his kitchen), while others were self-inflicted, such as the comedic fallout that occurred after he ended up on a TV game show.

Aslom has told his students these stories as a means of warning them of the dangers one can fall into during adolescence, and his students encouraged him to chronicle these events in the form of this book.

Aslom hopes to follow this teenage survival guide with its sequel: *Adulthood: A Guide To Surviving Working Life.*

www.ingramcontent.com/pod-product-compliance
Ingram Content Group UK Ltd.
Pitfield, Milton Keynes, MK11 3LW, UK
UKHW021837270325
456796UK00004B/497